GIRLS FALL LIKE DOMINOES

A. ROY MILLIGAN

Lock Down Publications and Ca$h

Presents

GIRLS FALL LIKE DOMINOES
A Novel by **A. Roy Milligan**

Lock Down Publications

Po Box 944

Stockbridge, Ga 30281

Visit our website @

www.lockdownpublications.com

Copyright 2020 by A. Roy Milligan

Girls Fall Like Dominoes

First Edition 2020
Printed in the United States of America

Lock Down Publications
Like our page on Facebook: Lock Down Publications @
www.facebook.com/lockdownpublications.ldp

Stay Connected with Us!

Text **LOCKDOWN** to 22828 to stay up-to-date with new releases, sneak peaks, contests and more…

Thank you.

Submission Guideline.

Submit the first three chapters of your completed manuscript to ldpsubmissions@gmail.com, subject line: Your book's title. The manuscript must be in a .doc file and sent as an attachment. Document should be in Times New Roman, double spaced and in size 12 font. Also, provide your synopsis and full contact information. If sending multiple submissions, they must each be in a separate email.

Have a story but no way to send it electronically? You can still submit to LDP/Ca$h Presents. Send in the first three chapters, written or typed, of your completed manuscript to:

LDP: Submissions Dept
Po Box 944
Stockbridge, Ga 30281

DO NOT send original manuscript. Must be a duplicate.

Provide your synopsis and a cover letter containing your full contact information.

Thanks for considering LDP and Ca$h Presents.

CHAPTER 1

Joy stood 5ft4, 135lbs with a nice round bubble butt and favored the singer Ciara, she had caramel skin just like her that glistened in the sun on a hot day. Her hair, well weave was long black and curly, she did her best trying to manage it herself because funds was tough.

At 6:45 in the morning, Joy was sitting in her car about a quarter mile away from her sister's house. She was waiting for her sister to leave so she could sneak up on the man of her sister's dreams. Joy had become angry and desperate about her situation. Her boyfriend, Daniel, had been the bread winner for the past couple years, but ever since the FEDS had indicted him five months ago, Joy had been having a hard time keeping up with a $4,000 dollar monthly mortgage and a $1,150 dollar car note. She was on the verge of losing everything and she knew she had to do something fast. She had the house up for sale, but no one was buying it because of the recession. Joy was 25 years old, but she hadn't worked a job in years because she always dealt with guys that made plenty of money in the streets. She sat back and waited until a little after seven when she saw her sister Hope backing out the driveway. Joy waited until her sister was no longer in sight before exiting her car and beginning to walk towards the home.

Hope and her boyfriend A'val were extra paid. A'val was a known drug dealer throughout Detroit. He only sold weed, but he was doing well for himself. After walking about ten feet, Joy stopped in her tracks, realizing she had just forgotten the bag that carried her clothes and a small pistol inside. Her plan was to tell A'val she needed to take a shower because she had an interview to go to. She was nervous grabbing her bag, but she still dialed her sister's house number and after four rings there was an answer.

"Hello?" A'val answered, sounding as if he was in a deep sleep.

"A'val, this Joy. You sleep?"

"Yeah, what up doe? Hope gone to work."

"Damn, she is?" Joy asked patiently as she waited for a response.

Finally, after about 10 seconds A'val said, "Yeah she at work, just call back later," he said, before hanging up in her face.

"Shit!" she said, stomping her feet. She quickly dialed the number again.

"He...llo."

"A'val why you hang up in my face? Open the door, I'm outside and I have an interview to go to. Let me come in and get ready," She said, not holding back.

CHAPTER 2

A'val didn't see anything wrong with letting her in, so he told her he was coming to unlock the door. A'val had been dealing with Hope for about six years now and he was really close to her family. There were never any problems between any of them and he managed to get along with them all. They knew he was a drug dealer, but they never held that against him.

Joy walked inside and headed straight to the bathroom. On her way, she noticed A'val walking to the bedroom wearing just a pair of black boxer shorts with nothing else. His light skin body was carefully sculpted where every cut and every lump for a muscle was perfectly defined.

"Do what you got to do and lock the door on your way out," he said, before closing the bedroom door.

"Ok, I just have to take a quick shower and I'm out," she responded, walking into the bathroom and closing the door.

A'val dove right back into bed and tried his hardest to go back to sleep, but then his cell phone started ringing. "Damn, hello?" he said answering the phone.

"What up? You up?"

"Yeah, I'm up, what up doe? Who dis, AJ?"

''Yeah, I need like five whenever you get up," AJ said.

"Alright, I'm about to get up in a second. I'll call you in a little while." A'val hung up and got out of bed, slipping on a pair of pants and a t-shirt as he walked to the living room shouting, "Joy!"

"What!"

"Make some breakfast before you leave please!"

"What you want?" She asked, opening the bathroom door in nothing but a towel. She didn't see A'val by the door so she walked out to where he was so he could see her.

A'val turned around and it kind of shocked him but he played everything cool. "Um, pancakes and eggs."

"Ok, how much you gone pay me?" she asked.

He laughed. "I got ten dollars for you."

"Make it twenty," she said smiling.

"Ok I got you," he said as he turned around and continued with what he was doing. He didn't want to give Joy no hint that he was checking her out while she was naked in a towel. Although he cheated on her sis, he respected and loved her to death.

"Do you know Angela?" she asked, thinking she would get a surprised look out of him, but it didn't happen.

"Naw, Angela who?" he asked, playing everything cool.

"The Angela you have pregnant." she said, smiling.

A'val stomach dropped when he heard those words flow from her mouth. "What? I don't know no Angela."

"Well she knows you. Lying is only going to make things worse so you might as well be honest before I tell Hope."

"Naw that's not necessary. I know that's your sister but let me tell her myself."

"How do you think she's going to feel about you having another girl pregnant? A white girl at that?" Joy asked, tilting her head.

CHAPTER 3

A'val was silent while looking at Joy in her eyes. He instantly sensed that Joy was up to something more than just a shower. "I'll tell her myself," he said.

"When? It better be today, because if you don't I will," she told him.

"Come on Joy don't do this shit, you know Hope will be crushed. I'm not even about to have that baby. I'm having her get an abortion."

Joy smiled to herself because she had already talked to Angela about that. "Well I'm telling my sister anyway because it's only right that she knows," Joy said, before she turned and walked away.

"Wait!" he shouted as he ran after Joy, grabbing her by the arm almost making her towel fall off.

"Don't touch me!' she yelled snatching away from him causing the skimpy towel to fly off of her.

A'val covered his eyes up. "Put your towel on please."

"Make me!" Joy said softly.

Confused by what he had just heard. "What you mean?"

"The only way I won't tell my sister is if you can pay some of my bills."

"What bills? Oh, you trying to black mail me now. That's fucked up."

"Yup." she spat.

"Well can you at least put your clothes on, or the towel, here," he said as he picked the towel up and covered her up.

"Call it what you want to call it."

"Damn you serious too. Why are you trying to do me like this?" he asked.

"Why are you doing my sister like this?" she replied and got no answer. "Exactly what I thought. Well I need $5000 dollars."

"What? I'm not giving you $5,000!"

"Ok," she said, heading to the bathroom to get her phone. "I'll just call and tell her right now."

A'val ran after her sticking his foot in the way before she could shut the door. He pushed it open and started wrestling her for the phone. Joy little self-versus A'val's 190 pounds of mostly muscle didn't stand a chance. It wasn't long before they were choking each other. Of course, his grip was a little bit more painful, so she let go and was reaching for her bag to grab her gun.

A'val had no clue she was reaching for a gun, but he did notice her reaching while screaming for him to let her go. He pulled her out of the bathroom before she could reach it and he took her back to the living room. She was kicking and gasping for air as he struggled, while still squeezing her neck. Finally, he threw her on the couch, "Damn bitch, chill the fuck out!"

CHAPTER 4

He touched his face and noticed blood from where she just scratched him. "I should fuck you up!" He told her as he stared at her nakedness while she was trying to catch her breath.

"I'm telling! You just fucked up!" she said breathing hard, trying to catch her breath.

"Look we got to work something out. I'm not about to tell Hope this shit, but $5,000 is just too steep, you are tripping."

"You got money! I know what you do!

A'val shook his head wondering why she was doing this. "Why you trying to blackmail me on this shit Joy, huh?"

Joy was quiet and tried covering herself up the best she could with her hands. Then took a deep swallow and said as she began to cry, " I'm about to lose everything. My house and car. I need the money so bad and I don't know what to do," she put her head and her lap and cried away.

A'val shook his head, he could not believe it. The recession had really hit some people hard to the point they were willing to do anything. "I'll help you, but you have to keep your mouth closed," he finally said.

Joy heard him but continued to cry, still on the couch naked. She felt disgusted and embarrassed of herself because she never seen this coming. She was the one that always had the nice car and newest designer bag, and now her life had taken a turn and she had no clue how to handle it. Daniel had been taking care of her with his hustle but now he was gone.

"But you gone have to sell the house and get rid of that BMW. You going to have to downsize and downgrade to something more affordable." he added.

"Ok." she said while drying her tears and shaking her head.

"Well, don't you have an interview to go to?" he asked.

She shook her head no and started crying again, even harder. A'val had no idea what was wrong with her now, so he went over and sat down next to her, then put his hand around her. "Stop crying, everything going to be ok, I told you I got you. What's wrong?"

She didn't say a word, just continued to cry for a few more minutes and as he was rubbing her back, she began to feel a warm feeling coming over her body as if things were really going to be ok and he was really going to help her out.

After getting her tears out, she just raised her head and looked up at him, admiring his light clear skin. His mustache and his thin beard were shaped as straight as she ever seen before on a man. After a few seconds of being hypnotized by his thick pink lips, she went in for a kiss, touching his lips, but he pulled back.

"What you are doing?" he asked as he backed up, but she kept coming towards him, kissing him again, this time locking lips with him and forcing her tongue inside his mouth. Then she started climbing on top of him, straddling him as her towel fell flat to the floor. She french kissed him aggressively while holding his face tightly with both of her hands while grinding her hips in his lap.

CHAPTER 5

"Wait, wait, wait," he said but she wouldn't stop, and he really didn't want to stop her. His dick was rising, his girl was gone, Joy was sexy, and she was butt ass naked in front of him.

"Shhh," she told him as she continued kissing his lips then his neck and chest. She was so turned on by how clean he smelled and how nicely built he was. His abs were bricked up, all eight of them. His arms were big and muscular, his pecks set just right, nipples were dark brown and the perfect size, and Joy could not wait to put it on him to make sure he kept his word. Joy loved her some chocolate men, but A'val had been on her radar for a long time now and today she was going to have her way, even if he was light skinned.

A'val pants came down with the help of them both and to his surprise Joy went to her knees and started sucking his dick, so he closed his eyes and laid his head back enjoying it. It wasn't long before she had his dick sticking straight up. She climbed back up on his lap and swallowed his dick inside her and started riding him, starting slow then speeding up and moaning in his ear. "Feel so good baby," she whispered.

CHAPTER 6

A'val was loving the way she felt inside, he couldn't believe this was happening. He never imagined having sex with anyone close to Hope. He always thought Joy was a pretty girl, but he never thought about taking it this far. Hope was gorgeous as well, looking just like her sister, just was a couple inches taller and a couple shades darker.

Ten minutes into their sex they were so into the moment they hadn't heard Hope come inside, but A'val eyes grew big as pineapples when he seen her when she came walking into the living room.

"What the fuck is this!" she shouted in rage. Her face turned red like a cherry and before A'val or Joy could say anything, Hope was racing towards them both with a vase she had snatched off the table. "You bitch!" she screamed swinging as hard as she could at A'val. He ducked and the vase went flying out of her hands and before she could grab something else, he tackled her to the ground.

Joy was scared out of her mind and she had no idea what to do or say. She was caught with her sister's man's dick inside of her and she couldn't think of anything to justify it.

"Bitch, I'mma kill you!" Hope shouted. "Get off of me!" she said trying to bite A'val's arm, but he would not let her go afraid of what she might do.

Joy ran for the bathroom and got all her stuff together, then raced out the door to her car and sped off. She drove towards home, shaking the whole way. She knew she had messed up and all she could do was cry her heart out. "Shit!' she shouted, beating on the steering wheel. She was not paying attention nor thinking and hadn't noticed the police lights behind her, but she heard the siren the second time it went off. "What the fuck?" she said as she stared through the rearview mirror. She had no idea what this officer could possibly want, but she pulled over to see.

"Good morning. License and registration please." The female officer requested.

"What did you pull me over for?" Joy had tears still falling from her eyes.

"Are you ok?"

"Yes, I'm fine. Why did you pull me over ma'am?"

"Well, I noticed you not wearing your seatbelt. And to my surprise you didn't try to slip it on neither," the officer said. She could tell Joy was going through something.

CHAPTER 7

J oy just sat back, shaking her head. She realized she wasn't wearing a seatbelt. She added, "Oh, I'm so sorry, it's been a horrible morning for me," she said, as she handed the officer her license and registration.

"Who's car is this?" The officer asked as she viewed the name of the registration and noticed that it didn't match the name on the license.

"My aunts."

"Very nice car, what a lucky niece you are."

"I guess... Can you hurry? I have somewhere to be," Joy stated with an attitude.

"Looking like that? I bet," The officer, said as she stared her in her face. She knew something was wrong with Joy. She could tell by the way she was dressed. Her clothes weren't even all the way on. She was wearing no bra, no shoes or socks and her hair was all over the place.

The officer told her she would be right back and she went to run her plates. A red flag was raised, and she noticed that the car had been in a traffic stop for drugs months ago and that made her want to search it to see if she could get lucky. First, she wrote Joy a seatbelt ticket then when she walked back to the window, she noticed Joy looking in the mirror trying to get herself together.

"Ms. Jones, here you go. That's your seatbelt ticket and I would like you to please step out of the vehicle. You look like you have been fighting and it's my job to make sure you're safe and that there is nothing funny going on."

"What? That's bullshit! I just got caught fucking my sister's boyfriend! Are you seriously going to make me step out of the car?" Joy snapped at her.

"Yes ma'am, and if you don't calm down, I'm going to have to cuff you. So please step out of the car and let me do a small search then I'll send you on your way."

Joy opened the car and stuck her foot out then reached for her bag to get her shoes. "I can't believe this. You see a black woman driving a $90,000 car and you think something has to be going on illegal."

CHAPTER 8

"**M**a'am please just step out of the car and follow me to the rear of the car," the officer said as she called for backup. After another officer arrived with a dog a few minutes later, Joy was cuffed and put in the back of the female officer's patrol car. Both of the officers began searching the car thoroughly and quickly discovered that Joy was armed with a gun but nothing else was found. The lady officer then went to the patrol car where Joy was waiting and asked, "Who's gun?"

"It's mine."

"You have permit for this?"

"Yea, it's in my glove department."

The two officers looked and found her CCW permit and they called in all the vendor numbers and Joy was clean. They had no choice but to let her go with just a seatbelt ticket. Joy smiled and shook her head as they uncuffed her. "Shit don't make any sense."

"Now you can go do what was so important," the lady officer said, pissed off that they couldn't arrest Joy for anything.

"Yeah, thanks a lot. You wasted a whole hour of my time, but it's cool because I'm self-made. You have a job to go back to. So, continue doing your job, and if you do it well enough, you might get yourself one of these someday, "Joy said, patting the car before closing her door and driving off.

When Joy arrived in her subdivision, she saw her silenced phone ring. It was her sister, she didn't answer. Then her mom was calling, and she still didn't answer. She was embarrassed, but she could care less because of the situation she was in. All her bills were past due, and no one was trying to help her, so she felt justified in doing what she had to do. Her phone continued to ring, but she paid it no attention. She walked into the house and noticed her house phone was ringing as well. Again, she ignored it. She sat down on the couch and was thinking about what A'val had told her about downsizing her lifestyle. It made perfect sense, but she was afraid of what others would think about her. Going from a BMW to a Charger, or a Grand Prix wasn't something she was interested in. All her girlfriends drove BMW's and Mercedes, so she wanted to continue driving them as well. The only problem was she couldn't afford it. She was missing her boyfriend and she badly needed him to call. Everything was a mess and she had been acting as if everything was fine, but she knew she had to finally tell him the truth.

CHAPTER 9

Joy sat for hours just watching her phone as it rang repeatedly, but as soon as she noticed the prison number calling, she answered it and accepted the call.

"I've been waiting for you to call," she said, sounding happy to talk to him.

"Whatsup baby? How are you?"

"I'm fine, well not really, but I'm ok." she said, stuttering.

There was silence on the phone for at least 5 seconds before he asked, "What's wrong?" sensing something wasn't right.

She took a deep breath and said, "I'm just tired of these bills. It's killing me and I don't know what to do."

"I thought everything was good. Did Jason give you that money for two months' rent?" He asked, referring to one of his partners.

"Yeah, he did," she said.

"And?"

"And what?" she asked.

"Did you pay the bills?"

"I paid the car note."

"What you do with the rest?"

She was silent and did not want to tell him the truth. "Joy, you heard what I asked you, what did you do with the rest?"

"Yeah, I heard you, I went shopping with Liah."

"You spent $9000 on shopping?" There was silence again because Joy didn't know what to say. This time he shouted, "Joy!!!"

"What? Stop yelling at me."

"What did you do with the money he gave you?"

"I got some rims for the car, we all got matching rims, Liah and all of us, so I didn't want to be left out."

"What? Left out? Joy, I am in prison. They sentenced me to 12 years! 12 years! You're going to lose everything, and you keep trying to keep up with them! You can't do what they do anymore! It's over, that shit is over!" he shouted trying to get through to her.

Joy didn't know what to say. She was so used to having everything she wanted, she didn't know what to do or how to change up. "Why did you leave me out here with nothing?" she asked, wanting to cry. "Where is all that money you were making? I know you have some left?" she said in tears.

CHAPTER 10

"**J**oy, they took everything. There is no money, I fucked up. I lost everything. I told you that before," he said, not able to believe everything he was hearing. "It's time to be smart baby. You can't live like that anymore. You have to work and go back to school now."

Joy was listening and she did not agree with him. She couldn't see herself working and school was a maybe. "No, No, I'm not punching no clock," she said as she began clearing up her tears.

"Well what are you going to do? You can't do what I did, so get that out of your head. What else you spent the money on?".

"I don't want to. I don't want to be where you are." she told him. "I bought clothes, shoes, Jewelry and them rims."

"Why didn't pay the bills? How did you think they would get paid?"

"I don't know."

"What the hell were you thinking? I got a lot of money put into that house and you about to lose it because you are doing stupid shit with money," he said getting angry now.

"I'm sorry, I don't know what to do," she said.

"Common sense should tell you to pay your bills before you go shopping and buying something so pointless."

"What's common to you is not common to everybody else." she said.

"You right. Listen, I'm not trying to hear all that smart shit coming out your mouth. Bottom line is you're going to have to start selling that stuff you don't need and get yourself into a position where you are comfortable. You might have to get a job as well Joy."

"I'll figure something out. Just let me think about it for a minute. Do you need anything?" she asked.

"Don't worry about me, I'm straight. You just worry about yourself right now," he said.

Although Joy wasn't his baby mother or wife, he had a lot of love for her, but he knew he'd messed her head up by spoiling her and showering her with the expensive lifestyle. He was just hoping and praying that he could help her learn some responsibilities and help better her situation.

The operator cut in informing them that they had one more minute to talk before the phone was about to hang up. They said their goodbyes and Joy felt a little better. She knew that she was going to have to sacrifice some things and she wasn't nearly ready to do that. She knew her friends would think differently about her and that scared her. Pontiac was small and everyone knew everyone, and she knew that downsizing her car would make everybody talk about her and she didn't want that. She didn't want to be labeled the girl that when her drug dealing boyfriend went to prison, she went downhill. She

22

did not want that title, so she knew that she had to do something with herself and fast. Joy's phone continued to ring and finally she answered. "Hello."

"What the hell is wrong with you sleeping with Hope's man!" her mom shouted through the phone making her feel like a little kid.

CHAPTER 11

"I..I don't know what I was thinking. I'm sorry," she said, feeling so bad inside.

"You're a fucking slut and you don't care about no one but yourself! Don't bring your ass over to my house! Stay away from me until you find your mind! You hurt your sister in one of the worst ways you could and that's unacceptable! Families don't do that to each other!" her mom yelled then she hung the phone up in Joy's face.

Joy dropped the phone and cried her heart out thinking about what her mom had just said. She knew her sister had to be hurt, and it hurt her to think about how her sister could possibly be feeling right now. A'val was all she had, and they had been together for so long. Joy laid on her marble kitchen floor and cried a puddle of tears inside an empty, huge five-bedroom house that was located in Bloomfield Hills. Her mind became more blank as she continued to cry, asking herself why she would do such a thing. She knew all hell was breaking loose with A'val and her sister, and it was all her fault. Her and her sister were so close before this day. They would go out to eat every week to see a movie and now that was all over. She knew Hope was not about to talk to her any time soon. Their relationship was over and thinking about it was like a sword stabbing her in the heart. As she cried on her kitchen floor, she felt a sharp pain in her chest. Her breathing became heavier and her tears became thicker and thicker. She had never experienced this much pain before, and it was nothing she wanted to feel again.

Joy had been asleep for a few hours and it was now 8 at night when she was awakened by a big noise. She got off the kitchen floor and started looking around. Confused about where it came from, until she heard it a second time, then a third, then finally a fourth. It was coming from outside. It didn't sound like a gunshot so she ran over to the window to see what was going on, but she couldn't see anything, then she ran to the door to see who it was in her driveway, but the car had sped off as soon as she went outside. *Who the hell was that and what were they doing in my driveway,* she said to herself.

She walked over to her car and saw that they had sliced her tires. "Fuck!" she shouted as she quickly ran back in her house to get her phone to call the police. She knew the only person that would do something like this was her sister. No one else knew where she stayed. She waited ten minutes before the police showed up, then she called her insurance company. She wasn't as mad because she felt as if she deserved it.

Right after she hung up her phone, she realized she had 41 missed calls, mainly from her sister's number and there were a couple other unfamiliar numbers as well. She called one back and a familiar voice answered that shocked her.

"Joy, what up doe? You good?" he asked.

CHAPTER 12

"I'm fine. What about you? Is she right there?" Joy asked.

"Naw, I wouldn't even have answered. You know she put me out so I'm staying up at this room," A'val said.

"No, I didn't know, I'm sorry about that."

"Don't trip, everything straight. She's not too mad at me. She only mad because I wasn't wearing a rubber, but she pissed at you."

"What?" Joy said with her mouth open.

"She seen you the whole time. She knew you had something up your sleeve. She seen you sitting outside. See I got Hope trained to watch her surroundings closely because of what I do."

"Wow...so she doesn't think you had nothing to do with it?"

"At first, she did. But she checked my phone and the home phone records and seen you had just called and that I never called you. But I told her that you said you just wanted to take a shower. She still mad at me but she ain't going nowhere."

"Wow," was all Joy could say.

"So, what up with you?" A'val asked.

"Nothing, I just woke up. Hope just left. She sliced my tires."

A'val laughed. "She's crazy. She was playing on my phone and shit. She's pissed off. I wish this would have never happened," he said.

Joy was silent. She didn't know how to take what he had just said.

"Hello?" He asked, thinking she had hung up.

"I'm here."

"So, what are you going to do about your bills?"

"I'm not sure right now, but you're going to help me, right?"

"Yeah, I got you. Just don't be running your mouth to nobody."

"Boy stop. I ain't about to say nothing to nobody about nothing I'm doing. "Nobody is trying to help me right now. I have a big house and a BMW that I can't afford at all. I'm going to lose everything in a minute, and nobody cares."

"What about your girls? Are they trying to help?" A'val asked.

"They don't know yet. I'mma go out to eat with them tomorrow, so I will tell them all then because they are my last resort. Daniel's side of the family don't even answer their phone for me anymore. Everything's just falling apart right now and it's just me trying to keep it together. I wish I could take back what happened earlier and maybe I could have just come right out an asked Hope for help instead of trying to have sex with you or black mail you. I just feel like shit right now."

"Yeah, I feel you, but it's done and over with. I told you I will help you out on that. I'll help you the best way I can," he said.

CHAPTER 13

"Yeah, I know, I just have a lot to think about. I think I'm going to have a yard sale tomorrow and sale everything inside this house except my clothes and stuff. I'll just sale the furniture and stuff and move into an apartment. I'm glad I'm not in debt. Daniel did help me get my credit up," she said.

"Well that's cool. Just call me on this number if you need something."

"Ok," she said, as they both hung up. Joy got up and jumped inside her Jacuzzi to soak her body. She sat there in deep thought for a few hours, drinking champagne thinking about the yard sale she would have tomorrow, first thing in the mourning.

A'val had just hung up the phone with Joy when he saw Hope calling him. "Hello."

"Where you at?" she asked.

"I'm at a hotel. What up doe?"

"Make sure you go to the clinic and get some results before you come back to this house," she said calmly, very much in control of herself now.

A'val could tell she had been drinking then he noticed the noise in the background. "What's that, where you at?"

"Home with my girls," she said.

"I'll go to the clinic tomorrow morning. I really am sorry for what happened Hope. I swear I am, and I feel like shit for doing that to you."

Hope didn't say anything, she just bust out crying, "Why would you do something like that? You really don't love me A'val! You fucked my sister! What am I supposed to do? I can't be with you no more, you embarrassed me A'val! Do you even know how I feel right now?" she said, crying even harder through the phone. "I feel like killing you both, but neither one of you is worth going to jail for. I thought you loved me A'val! I really did!" She shouted and could not stop crying.

"I do baby I'm sorry. I really don't know what to do besides say I'm sorry and I would never do that again. I promise. I didn't mean to hurt you. You know I would of never came at your sister like that."

CHAPTER 14

"**A**'val, when I walked in, your dick was inside her with no rubber on. How many bitches do you fuck without a rubber? You're just nasty! You are disgusting to me right now! I swear, if I have anything when I go to this doctor, I never want to talk to you again A'val and I mean that. I'm done," she said as she continued to cry. Finally one of her friends heard her crying and came and took the phone from her and hung it up in Aval's face.

A'val was crushed as well. He even shed a few tears while blowing two blunts of Kush by himself. He stayed at the hotel all by himself until the next morning. He then got up to the sound of his ringtone. He had about four people waiting that wanted weed. He told them all to come up to the hotel and they did. He sold them all the pounds of weed he had up there with him and sent them on their way. Later he went to the clinic to find out he was clean, so the first thing he did was call Hope to tell her. She told him she was clean as well and that it would probably be best that he stayed in a hotel room for a few days because she could not stand to be around him. He begged her to come home but that didn't work. Hope was pissed and she wanted to beat her sister up so bad, but her mom told her not to.

The next morning Joy was up and dressed and she did not feel like having a yard sale especially after getting her tires fixed and the headache with all that, so she called one of her close friends to meet with her for breakfast. They both met about an hour later at a nice restaurant located in Southfield. When Joy arrived, she parked her car next to Mesha's. Mesha was driving a smoke grey BMW 745 with 22" rims as well. Mesha's boyfriend was another big drug dealer from Detroit and he spoiled her just like Daniel spoiled Joy. They were all part of the same circle and they all took good care of the females they dealt with.

Mesha stepped out of her car as soon as she saw Joy. Mesha stood 5"8, light skin, red bone, thick in the hips, big round booty, very big titties due to the surgery she just had on them. "Hey girl!" Mesha shouted and smiled with her eyes wide open.

Although Joy wasn't as excited as she was, she tried to act like she was. "Heeey slut!" Joy joked, while hugging her. "I like that dress with them pumps." Joy told her while admiring the black pumps she wore with the black tight-fitting dress that was cut all over, revealing different parts of her skin.

"Thank you, girl I just bought it yesterday on sale too."

"Who is that?" Joy asked, as she was distracted by a guy that had just arrived driving a navy blue Cadillac XL truck.

"I don't know him and I'm not trying to know him." Mesha said, turning to walk inside. "I don't fuck niggas that drive Cadillacs no more. I'm past that," she said, switching as she walked away.

Joy noticed the guy was looking at her but then turned away.

CHAPTER 15

"Come on Joy! Standing up there looking like you lost," Mesha jokes.

Joy laughed and started walking inside. "Girl you are so silly. He was a cutie. I thought he was about to stop."

"He's broke, forget him."

"You be killing me with all that. Every guy doesn't have to have a Mercedes or Bentley to have money. Trae got you over there all screwed up."

Mesha laughed. "It doesn't have anything to do with Trae. He just taught me how to see through these petty drug dealers. Homeboy in the truck is not moving no real weight."

"Mesha, I don't care what he is moving. He's cute."

"Yes you do," Mesha said quickly and they both started laughing. They were seated by the window and Joy was looking outside to see if the guy was about to come inside, but she noticed him just sitting out there, talking on the phone.

"So what's up with the yard sale? I called Armoni and Phia, they should be pulling up in a second," Mesha said.

"Oh you did, cool. The yard sale? Well you know it's been difficult since Daniel left so I was going to get like an apartment or something. I don't want to stay in that big house by myself you know? All them bedrooms and I only be inside mine and the kitchen."

"Well I can understand that. How is everything else going?"

"It's ok. Money has been an issue, but things will get better," Joy told her.

Armoni arrive in her Mercedes, then Phia came behind her in a Mercedes. They both had 22" Chrome rims.

"There they go right there," Joy said pointing at them through the window.

Armoni was Mexican with long black hair with a nice body. Phia was a red bone just like Mesha and she also had a nice body. All four of them had pretty faces and carried themselves like they were allergic to broke guys. They all hugged and kissed each other's cheeks, then sat down to eat and talk about everything. Joy was kind of like an outcast because when she informed them about her situation it was like they didn't care to hear it because they were so caught up on what they had going on. She was shocked because they had been knowing each other for about 5 years now. Joy thought they was going to be trying to help her, but it was like they didn't care. Phia told her if she needs somewhere to sleep, let her know and Armoni agreed before they both laughed. What they thought was funny was not a joke to Joy.

"Excuse me for a second, I have to use the restroom," Joy said before she left the table alone.

"Girl, Joy isn't about to have that car too much longer," Mesha said.

"She better find her another baller," Phia said.

CHAPTER 16

"That's her problem. She knew she was supposed to be preparing for this day. I have my own money saved up right now for when Rino goes down. And we all know that day is coming," Armoni said.

"I know that's right. She should know that her situation is part of the game. One day you could be winning and the next, lose everything," Mesha said.

"And unfortunately for her, we are still winning!" Phia said, as she put her drink in the air. "Are you gonna give her some money Mesha?" Phia asked.

"I don't have anything to give right now. My husband is trying to start a business. We don't have any extra money right now. I don't have extra money put to the side like Armoni little slick ass over there," she joked, and they all started laughing again.

"Girl, I'm not playing out here. Rino talking about having a baby. I told him we are not having anything, unless you can promise me you are going to stop moving the bag. If he gets a business or something maybe I will go for it. And Rino is getting too much money to not invest his money and I'm not going for that," Armoni said.

"Why do you want to start a business then?" Mesha asked.

"I don't know how that shit go. Rino is my business. He pays very well." They all started laughing again.

"Oh my god, did you hear what Joy did though?" Phia asked.

"No, what?" Mesha asked, curious.

"She fucked A'val, her sister's boyfriend for some money," Phia said.

"What?" Mesha said with her mouth wide open.

"You are lying!" Armoni said surprised as well.

"I swear. One of her sister's friends is my cousin so you know she told me everything. I couldn't believe it," Phia said.

Joy came back and sat down and everyone was speechless. "Damn, was something in the food? Joy asked, smiling. "Everybody quiet," she said.

"I'm full," Mesha said, taking a drink of water.

"Me too," Armoni added.

"So, are we all going out later?" Mesha asked.

"Of course."

"Yeah, why not?"

"Maybe, I'm not sure. I have a lot to do. Where y'all going to be at, I might come out?" Joy asked.

"I don't know yet, just call me around seven and I'll tell you, we should have it figured out by then, "Mesha said.

"Ok, that's fine. Well I have to go so I'll see y'all later," Joy said feeling an awkward vibe.

"What time is the yard sale?" Phia asked.

"I'll call you if I have it or not," Joy said before she was out the door.

"That bitch didn't even leave her money for her food." Phia said. Armoni laughed.

"She probably doesn't have it, I'll pay for it." Mesha said.

CHAPTER 17

J oy left and called A'val. He was the only person that was willing to help her or give her money. Everyone else besides Daniel was just making things worse. She wished that she could call her mother, but her mother was mad at her. She felt as if she had no one. She had never felt this lonely in her whole life. And when she needed for Daniel to be there for her, he was away in prison.

"Hello."

"A'val, what are you doing? You up?" Joy asked.

"Yeah, what up doe? I'm on my way to give these results to your sister."

"What results?" she asked.

"Because we didn't use a condom, she wants me to show her the paper saying that I don't have anything."

Joy laughed. "That's my sister for you."

"Right. I'mma give her what she wants though. What's up with you, is everything ok?"

"No, it's not."

"Well look, I should only be about 20 minutes here, meet me at that hotel I threw my cousin's party at last year. Do you remember?"

"Yeah, I'll be there, you might beat me there. I'm coming all the way from Southfield."

"Ok, I'll see you in a minute." he said before he hung up. He knew Joy had to be in a horrible state of mind and he knew that he could not spend much time around her because if Hope found out it was over. So, he called a friend of his that lived in Traverse City which was north from Detroit. He was a heavy-set guy named Stuff, but a nice guy and he was getting a lot of money in the northern area from all the white people. A'val figured if he could get him to talk to Joy about her situation, she would be good. And since Stuff was single, they might like each other. A'val knew Stuff was a good dude and could show Joy some new ways to make money. Stuff showed A'val how to start his two cell phone stores about three years ago.

"What's up A'val?" Stuff said as he answered his phone.

"What up doe? I got this lil chick I need you to holla at about starting her a business or something. She's a cutie man, you might like her too."

Stuff laughed. "Who is this girl and what's in it for me?"

"She is actually my sister in law. I really need you to do it for me as a favor. I kind of got her in a fucked up situation and I need her out the way for a minute so I can fix it." A'val said.

"Oh, this is family?"

"Yeah, my sis."

"Ok, so?"

"I was thinking maybe I can send her up there if she willing to."

"Well, let me know after you find out or I could just talk to her on the phone and see if I can have her come."

"I was thinking if I send her up there and she sees how you are living up there on the beach with boats and shit, she would be inspired to want to get herself together."

CHAPTER 18

"**W**ell, leave that up to me. I'll take care of that, just give her my number and when she calls, I'll see where her mind is at and we'll go from there." "Ok cool, thanks Stuff. I'll holla at you later."

"You welcome, anytime. How are the shops going?"

"Man, they are doing really good, I can't complain at all really."

"Okay A'val keep your head up and take it easy."

After they hung up, he headed back to the hotel to meet Joy. As soon as he arrived, he saw her sitting in her BMW. *Damn that car out cold,* he said to himself.

They met each other in the lobby then both headed to the floor where his room was. "So what's up?" he asked.

"I just don't know what to do," she said as she sat down on the brown sofa and crossed her legs.

"Did you have the yard sale yet?" he asked.

"No. I don't have anyone to help me."

"Why not, you have friends. What's up with them? Why didn't they help you?" he asked, as he walked over to the glass table to pour himself a drink. "Thristy?" he asked, holding a bottle of Ace.

"Please, just a little though," she replied. "I mentioned it to my friends this morning and they acted like they didn't care. They just said things like, everything will be ok, and it will work itself out. Stuff like that, you know. None of them asked me if I wanted some help or needed some help."

"Well did you ask for help?"

"Not really, but somewhat."

"See, you should have asked. You can't assume they will just volunteer. After all, why would they?"

"Because I would for them. I would help them if they boyfriend was in prison and I knew one of them didn't have a job."

"Everybody not like you though. For one, they could be jealous of you and want to see you doing bad."

"Naw, they not like that," she said.

"I'm just saying."

"I just think they think I have money or something. You right though. I'm going to just ask each of them to borrow some money and see."

A'val shook his head up and down. "That's all you could do. If they say no, then you know what's up."

"Right. Ok be quiet really quick, let me call," she said, picking her phone up, first going to Mesha's number.

"Haaaaay girl" Mesha answered.

A. ROY MILLIGAN

"Hey, what you doing?"

"Nothing, just walked in the door."

"I need a favor. I wanted to ask you earlier but not in front of Phia. She talks too much."

"What is it?"

CHAPTER 19

"**I** need to borrow some money, I'm about to lose my house and my car. You know I wouldn't ask if I didn't need it. I'll pay you back as soon as I can. Give me about two months."

"I don't know girl. Right now is a bad time because Trae has so much going on right now."

"Damn ok, well if something comes up and you can help me, call me please."

"You know I will," Mesha said, but Joy did not believe her.

"What happened?" A'val asked when he saw her hang the phone up.

"She doesn't have it. I guess I'm going to call Armoni. I know she has it," she said as she dialed her number but Mesha had already called her and told her, so she did not pick up the phone. Joy left a message letting her know it was important and to call her back asap "She didn't answer."

"Your friends sound like they're not real friends."

"They cool. They just have things to do."

"So, what are you going to do? Have you looked for a job?" he asked.

"I'm not about to work for anyone," she said.

"Well what are you going to do, start a business?"

"That's what I was thinking about. I rather do that then go work for someone else," she said.

"How do you know?" "How

do I know what?"

"How you know you'd rather start a business then work for someone else if you haven't ever done either one?"

"Because I'm not good at taking orders. I'll do the opposite of what someone tells me on purpose." They both started laughing.

"Well I have a friend that can teach you some things about business. He helped me."

"I'll just go to school for business," she said.

"Well put this number in your phone just in case. He's a good dude. Call him if you have questions about anything. He will help you."

"Ok, thanks I'll keep this," she said and took the piece of paper with his number on it and stuck it in her purse.

They talked for a couple hours and Joy was out of there by noon to have her yard sale. She moved everything out of her house by herself. She even posted some flyers up on a few light poles she had made herself. By 6:00pm everything was gone, and she had just under $6000. If Daniel knew she had sold everything that cheap he would be pissed. She had even sold some of her clothes and shoes. Now she was looking for someone to buy her rims. She called A'val asking him to call a couple of his guys to try to sell them, but no one was interested. So, she called a guy she was dating before.

CHAPTER 20

"**D**amn, girl I thought you fell off the face of the earth," he said when he picked up the phone.

She laughed. "Hey, I'm trying to sell my rims. They 22 inch Forgiatos. Do you know anyone that would buy them?"

"How much you want?"

"Um, for you," Give me $4000. They brand new. I paid $7,500 for them," she said.

"Bring them thru and I'll cash you out for them. I'll put them on my Lexus," he said.

"Oh, you have a Lexus now?"

"Yea something light for now. You remember where I stay?"

"On Joy Road. right?"

"Yeah, when can you come thru?" "I

have to get them taken off first."

"Naw you good, my mans do all that. Just come through.

Make sure your other tires are in your trunk. I'll have him get you together."

"You want me to come right now?"

"Yeah if you can."

"I'm supposed to go out to eat so your boy going to have to hurry exchanging the tires."

"I got you. Can I eat that pussy while you wait?"

She laughed not wanting to curse him out afraid of the fact of losing her sale. "I'll think about it." she said.

She headed to Detroit to Joy Road where she remembered he was. She called him as soon as she arrived. The sun was shining and the whole street was crowded. Young kids were dancing in the streets doing all the popular dances. People were sitting on their porches smoking and playing cards listening to the latest rap or R&B songs. People were everywhere and Joy didn't see a Lexus in sight. She had called him twice, but she got no answer. So, she figured she would just park in front of the house she remembered being at. She didn't know if she should just walk up to the door because she didn't want to run into one of his female friends. She sat and waited about ten minutes before she noticed a young teen knock on her window. He couldn't be any older than 17 years old. She let her window down to see what he wanted, and he grabbed her hair and smacked her in the face with his gun. Joy began to scream as he unlocked her door and pulled her out the car. Two other guys were with him as well and she hadn't seen them. When they pulled her out the car, she grabbed her purse and was trying her hardest to get to her gun.

"Give me this purse bitch!" One guy said as he snatched it from her then jumped in her car and sped off. She laid in the middle of the street crying and bleeding from the side of her forehead until a lady ran to her rescue.

"Are you ok baby?" she asked as she helped her to her feet. She was short, kind of chubby, wearing red lipstick with very short hair.

"Yeah, I'm ok." Joy said.

CHAPTER 21

"Come on in here. Let's get you cleaned up."

"You have a phone?" Joy asked.

"Yup, no problem," the lady said. She brought Joy inside her house where she lived by herself. She got Joy a warm wet towel then gave her a phone to call whoever she needed to call. Before she could dial the number, a little girl was at the door holding a cell phone in her hand. Joy saw her first and she ran to the door.

"They must have dropped this. Here you go. Just give me five dollars," the little girl said.

"Bre you better get your little ass away from here!" The lady shouted after she snatched the phone out of her hand and handed it to Joy.

"Thank you so much." Joy said, smiling. First, she called the police and made a police report then she called Mesha but got now answer. She then tried to call Armoni and Phia but they didn't answer either. She didn't understand why they weren't answering because it was almost time for them to go and eat. She wanted to call her mom or her sister, but she knew they were mad at her that they probably wouldn't care. So, she called A'val and he answered on the first ring.

"What up doe?"

"Someone just carjacked me. I need you to come get me please," Joy said trying not to cry.

"What? Where? Where you at?"

She told him where she was, and he told her he was on his way. By the time he arrived. Joy had just finish talking to the police about what happen. When she seen A'val coming she jumped in the car with him.

"Damn, what happened? You good?"

"Hell no! They took all my money!" she said in a squeaky voice before crying.

"Damn, was it a lot?"

"Yeah! Over $6000!" she told him.

"Why are you riding with all that money?"

She was quiet for a second and finally said, "I don't know. But that was all my money from my yard sale. I just sold almost all my furniture in my house." she said crying and wiping the tears from her eyes. "Just take me home please. I'll make an insurance claim tomorrow," she said.

A'val drove her all the way home. "I thought you sold all the furniture. What are you about to sleep on?"

"I don't care, I guess the floor. This is crazy. I can't believe this is happening to me."

"Look, let me pay for you a room until you figure something out. I'll give you what you lost but you have to get yourself together," he told her.

Joy then told him about the guy she was supposed to meet, and he told her that she probably was setup.

CHAPTER 22

O ne month later

A'val was on his way to Joy's apartment. Him and Hope was still working on their relationship, but they were back together. A'val had 30 pounds in the trunk and he was going to meet one of his workers in her apartment complex. Soon as he arrived, he seen his homeboy waiting on him in a black Ram 1500 pickup truck. He delivered the packages inside two big duffle bags then made his way to Joy's apartment.

"What up doe?" he said when he walked in.

"Hey."

"Damn, you look like Cierra for real with your hair like that," he said as he noticed her dark blonde colored hair hanging way past her shoulders.

Joy smiled. The past month, she had been still going through stuff and she was now driving a 4 door Malibu. She was still not working but she was going to school for business. Her friends Mesha, Armoni and Phia didn't even answer their phones for her ever since she had picked them all up from the airport in her Malibu. They knew she had hit rock bottom and they didn't want anything to do with her. She had lost her house and her car. All Joy's money had been coming from A'val. A'val was looking out for her until she got on her feet like he said he would. He had also aborted the baby he had on the way, but he still helped Joy with no strings attached. Joy was doing really bad and the only thing she knew to do was to go to college.

"Did you ever get to call Stuff?" A'val asked while counting all the money he had just got.

"Who?"

"Stuff. Remember I told you that I had a good friend that knew a lot about business?"

"Oh yeah. Naw, I didn't call him. I'll learn it through school. This the real stuff," she said.

"Just call him and see what he's talking about. He can be your little friend and probably spend a little money on you."

"No, I'm not talking to him for no money."

"Well just talk to him and see what he can help you with. Tell him you are going to school for business."

"I might, I don't know A'val."

"You need to do something. You need to make something happen for yourself. I can't continue to just give you money. I feel like as long as I'm doing it, you are going to be slacking."

"See I knew this was coming. You know what A'val, fuck you too. You just like the rest of them. Don't pay my rent no more. I don't care! Get out!" she shouted.

CHAPTER 23

A'val was shocked but he just cleaned up his money and left. He was tired of feeling sorry for her because he sensed that she wasn't trying to do anything with herself. She didn't want to get a job. And she knew nothing about responsibilities. Her mom had turned on her and so did her sister and she didn't know how to make it better. She stayed in her apartment for two months straight without paying rent. She still didn't have a job and she barely was able to put gas in her car. She had to carpool other students just to get gas money. And she went on dates with all kind of guys just to eat. As long as she ate one meal a day, she was fine. She had started losing weight and she was becoming more stressed out. Daniel had even backed off of her, she had recently heard that he had a daughter that was one years old. She went to go see him and he confirmed that it was true with no hesitation. Daniel was shocked at how bad Joy was looking when she came into the visiting room. When she asked him if it was true that he had a baby, he said yes. That pissed her off so bad that she slapped him, spit in his face then stormed out of the visiting room. On her way to her car she again realized her life was falling apart. She no longer had a place to live, a boyfriend, a family, a friend, a home, or a cell phone. She had just bought a minute phone. She figured she didn't use it much anyway so why pay a high bill. All she had was herself and a car. She dropped out of college and she began living out of her car for three days before she could no longer take it. She broke down and called her mom.

"Hello," her mom answered, and she heard crying instantly and knew that it was her daughter from the feeling in her chest and stomach. It had been months since she had heard from her Joy. But it had felt like forever.

"Joy, baby is this you?"

Joy could barely talk or breathe. She was so happy to hear her mother's voice, she shouted through tears, "Yeah, it's me mama."

"Are you ok baby? Joy?" Her mom asked, as she tried to stay as calm as possible.

Joy continued to burst out with tears. "Ma, I want to come home. Please!" she begged as she cried even harder.

Her mom's natural reaction was to accept her, and she wasn't going to fight it. She knew that Joy had to be in a bad place in her life at this moment and she was not going to turn her back on Joy, "Come home baby. Come home," her mom said, still calm but now shedding tears for her daughter.

Joy couldn't say a word. All she could do is cry. She was so happy her mom accepted her back. After crying for about five more minutes she hung up with her mom and headed over there. Her mom accepted her with open arms but cried just seeing how bad her daughter looked. She was as skinny as a broomstick. She had lost a lot of weight and she didn't even look the same.

CHAPTER 24

The next morning Joy and her mom went job hunting and they talked about everything. "I don't mind you staying with me, but you have to get a job and save your money. Then I'll help you get your own place." her mom said.

"That shouldn't be hard. I can do that." Joy said, smiling.

"No boys in my house. Well you are 25 years old, the guys you deal with should have their own house anyway."

"Right. Well I'm not dealing with any guys right now. I'm just trying to focus on myself right now," she said.

Her mom was glad to hear that. "Well, good."

They drove to several places filling out applications and one guy wanted to interview her right on the spot. It happened and Joy got the job working for $8.00 an hour answering a phone at a local barber shop in Detroit. Joy thought about that job all night and she could not wait to go to her first job she had ever had. She got up early in the morning to take a shower and got herself dressed to impress.

She was there at 9am on the dot ready to work. "Hi Steve!" she said, smiling when she walked through the door looking good, wearing a new dress she had just got because she was unable to fit the clothes she had. She had lost way too much weight.

Steve was an Arab guy that owned the barber shop. He was about 200 pounds and he had a nice height to him to stretch those pounds out. You could tell that he went to the gym faithfully. "Hey mama. How are you this morning?" he replied.

"I'm fine, ready to work that's all," she said.

"Good, I like your spirit already. Now let me warn you before anyone gets here. There will be a lot of guys trying to talk to you and date you. That's totally up to you but make sure you don't bring no drama to my establishment. I prefer you not to mess with my customers because it can cause confusion, but I know I can't stop it, but be aware of the things that could happen. This is why I fired the last girl. She had slept with so many of the guys, they stopped coming in to get their hair cut, trying to avoid her."

"You don't have to worry about me. I won't even give one my number," she said.

"Good. Well no need to worry about anything right?"

"Right."

Joy, later that day seen so many men she wouldn't mind talking too, it was crazy. She wanted to take back what she had said earlier. These guys were mostly ballers that was coming in. They were driving every car you can think of, over $50,000 and Joy was in heat. She hadn't had sex since the encounter with A'val, but today her juices were flowing. She felt like she had her life back.

CHAPTER 25

A month went by and Joy had been picking her weight back up. Her booty was showing again but this time it was bigger, and her waist was smaller. She looked healthy again and she had been doing very well. Her mom was fine with her living with her until Joy started coming in late, shopping all the time and calling off from work to be with a guy she had met from the barber shop. He was a drug dealer from Atlanta, but he showed his face in Detroit a lot and every time he was in town, he was calling Joy. Joy had gone out with him twice, but tonight he asked her to fly to Atlanta with him for a day. He flew her in, and she arrived in Atlanta about 2am. The plan was for her to fly back home the next day.

"What sup shawty?" Pooh asked when he saw her. He had told her not to pack because he was going to take her shopping.

"Hey!" she said, smiling and hugging him.

He walked her outside and put her bags in the trunk of his Range Rover then they headed to the mall. He let Joy get whatever she wanted which wasn't much. He had only spent $875.00. He expected to spend $2000. So far, he was doing good. He then drove her to where he lived. It was a gated community with eight big houses that were set in one big circle. They were all well over a million dollars each.

Joy wasn't surprised or impressed. This was nothing new to her. When she was with Daniel, he took her around many people that had plenty of money, plus the house she had previously moved from was almost a million.

"This is nice. Is this where you live?" she asked.

"Yeah, this one of my spots. You can take a shower here and do whatever you need to do shawty," he said with his country accent and a mouth full of gold.

Joy didn't really like the gold, but she was accepting it for now. It was still dark outside when they arrived but there were so many lights on outside of the complex you could see everything clearly.

"I'll take a shower later, I'm going to get some sleep first." she said.

"Ok, that's cool too, don't trip." he said, driving into his garage.

They then went into the house and Joy eyes lit up. This guy had marble everything. She hadn't ever seen this much marble. She had thought she had a lot of marble in her old house, but he was putting her to shame.

"Damn," she said, thinking out loud.

"What's up?" he asked as he was busy turning on lights.

"This is nice," she said, before she started screaming her lungs out.

CHAPTER 26

Pooh was hit in the head by one guy dropping him to the floor and two other guys came from behind Joy and choked her up with their hand around her mouth.

"Shut up bitch before I silence you myself!" One gunman said. She instantly went silent. She was scared and she didn't know what to do or think.

"I don't know him. Please just let me go and I swear ya'll don't have to worry about me." she said after they threw her on the couch.

Two of the guys had already dragged Pooh away.

"You good, just sit tight," the gunman said. "This ain't got shit to do with you." he told her.

All she could do is just stare at him although she couldn't see a thing through the black ski mask he was wearing. She sat there silent while the other guys were doing whatever they were doing to Pooh. All she heard was screams from Pooh. They were trying to get him to give them money.

Pooh gave them money hoping they would not kill him since

he didn't see their face but they did. He was shot three times in the chest and that scared Joy so badly she got up and tried to run but the guy tackled her. Since she screamed, he put the gun to her head and started threatening her until the other guys came downstairs ready to go.

"Kill that bitch bro!" one yelled.

"Nooo, please don't!" she shouted. "I don't know nothing, I swear I don't!" she said, crying her heart out.

"Shoot her bro!" he shouted again.

"She straight man," the guy said that was holding her at gunpoint the whole time. "Did ya'll handle what we came for?" he asked.

"Yeah bro! You just gone let that bitch live?"

"Get the fuck out of here, get the car." he ordered them, and they did. "Today's your lucky day beautiful. Stay away from drug dealers." he told her. "Next time you'll be dead too," he said before he got up and ran out the door, leaving her with her heart in her panties.

After waiting for ten minutes she ran out of the house still crying and hoping no one had seen her. She had to walk about six miles before she was able to get service on her cell phone to call a cab. She paid her way all the way to the airport then back home on a plane.

CHAPTER 27

When she arrived back in Michigan, she had seven dollars to her name left. She called her mom to come get her and her mom gave her a big lecture about how she was only giving her a month to get her stuff together. Joy wasn't trying to hear it. She was scared for her life and she did not want to tell her mom what had just happened. It was happening all over again for a second time. Her life was beginning to fall apart again, and nothing was going right. She wasn't going back to her job because she was scared, everyone knew Pooh and she didn't want to be in the middle of nothing. The rest of the month she continued to look for another job and she finally got one, flipping burgers for $6.50 an hour. She worked a week and quit without telling her mom. She then started working at a place that sold Tacos. That only lasted a week and two days. She could not handle the way her bosses would talk to her. She felt the money wasn't worth staying. Two months had passed and Joy still could not keep a job. She would get fired for being late on her first day, or not wanting to wear a hair net. It was always something. She knew soon she would be meeting face to face with her mom but her mom gave her some extra months and all Joy did was party, drink, and have sex with people that promised her to be a part of a magazine, a modeling career or a spot in a video. She had been running into some great people while mingling but they sold her dreams because they knew she would fall for it.

It had been about five months now and her mom came into her room about 1:45pm in the afternoon and noticed that Joy was sleeping. She was fed up. Joy was taking everything for granted. Her mom had even been going over to Hope house to see and chat with her just because Hope didn't want to come over because she knew Joy was staying there.

"Joy!" her mom yelled but Joy didn't move. She had partied hard last night, and she didn't get home until five in the morning. "Joy! Get your ass up!" her mom shouted again as she slapped Joy in her head twice.

"Mom, what?" Joy asked out of a deep sleep.

"Get up and pack your shit! I'm done, you're on your own! I tried and tried to help you, but I see you are not trying to do nothing with yourself!"

"Mom, I can't even find a job." she said as she raised up.

"Ugh, you smell like a drunk!" her mom said after she noticed her breath.

"I'm leaving, I'll be back around seven. Leave my key on the counter and pack your shit and get out!" her mom said, then she slammed the door closed and left the house.

CHAPTER 28

Joy was pissed and still drunk. She had about 25 dollars in her pocket and she didn't know what she was going to do. She called Mesha, Armoni and Phia, crying and asking if she could stay with them for a while, but they all had the same answer, that they were about to go to the Bahama's with their men. They had no sympathy for Joy's situation, and she realized then that they were not her friends. She packed, left and she was back to living out of her car again. But this time she felt even worse. It was one morning when her car acted as if it didn't want to start. Her car was dying and all she had, that she felt was worth anything was her body, and her looks. Stripping and prostitution crossed her mind, but she could not bear the thought. She didn't want to ruin herself like that. She had met some new friends while living with her mom but she did not want to go to them without any money, or a job. For all they knew, she was doing pretty good.

Her fifth night of staying in her car she knew she had to do something fast, but she had no clue what to do. She began thinking about everything in her life including when Daniel was free. She used to live the lavish life people dream about living and now she was nothing. She had hit rock bottom for a second time. This time harder than ever. All she could afford to eat was a pack of noodles. And she ate that without even cooking it. Since they were only 16 cents it worked for her but this was not the life she wanted for herself. Sitting in her car all day and spending most of her time walking around the mall wasn't fun. She was meeting guys and she wanted to go stay with them, but she knew if she did that, she would never get the answers she is looking for. She had filled out applications but there was no way to contact her because she had no phone. Her hair began to look so bad she just started staying in her car with a notebook and a pencil. She wrote all her goals down, then she started writing a book about her past experiences. Writing a book took up so much time, the days eventually would just fly by. All she would do was move from place to place. She sat for seventeen days writing a book. The book was her therapy. She ate noodles and wrote every day. She had lived off under 25 dollars for nearly a month.

CHAPTER 29

I t had now been 23 days and she hadn't taken a shower in 16 days. The smell of her car had changed to a smell comparable to a women's locker room. It smelled as if someone had died. She started taking small wash ups at the same restaurant she was parked near and when she was on her period, she made her own pad to stop the bleeding. She used plastic with a lot of toilet paper.

Today around midnight she had just finished her last chapter of her book. "Yes!" she said.

"The streets going to love this." she said. Then she looked at her watch, at the date and time and realized how long she had been living in her car. "Fuck!" she said beginning to cry. She hadn't cried in a while because the book kept her so busy but now everything was hitting her again. She didn't know what to do next. She thought about the guy Stuff, that A'val told her to call and wondered if the offer was still on the table. She then started to look for his number in her phone remembering that she had saved it under something that was easy to remember. She found it and she promised herself she was going to call him from a payphone tomorrow morning offering him partnership in her book project.

The next morning around six, Joy was fully awake. She could not stop thinking about what she would say to Stuff if he answered the phone. She then went to a gas station bathroom and stayed inside for about two hours. She washed herself up about ten times and she fixed herself up, looking her best. Then she put on a nice dress. She had done her hair, washed and blow dried it and all she had to do was go to the pay phone.

When she left the bathroom, she left the door wide open because the smell was so bad and the perfume that she had sprayed just made it worse.

She then went to the phone and dialed his number.

"Yuup!" he answered.

"Hi Stuff, I'm Joy, A'val is my brother in law. He told me to call you because business is the topic," she said.

"Oh yeah, I remember him saying something about you some months back. What did you say your name was again?"

"I'm Joy."

"Ok Joy, So what's up?"

CHAPTER 30

"**W**ell I was wondering if you wanted to go in on a partnership thing. I have this book that I wrote and I-"

He cut her off, "Hold on, did you say a book?"

She got excited hoping that this would be good. "Yeah, a hood classic guaranteed!" she said.

"I'm sorry lil mama but I'm not into that. I don't know anything about getting published."

"That's what I'm calling for, just give me a chance and I'll do all the research necessary. I just need you to invest in me."

He was quiet thinking to himself rather or not this would be worth it. "Naw mama, that ain't something I'm trying to do. I run a lot of shit. I'm into franchising and stuff like that."

Joy didn't even know what franchise meant. "Oh, well can you just help me please. I really want to learn, I don't even have anywhere to stay, no money, or nothing. I'll work for free for you if I have too."

"A'val let you be out there like that." Stuff asked becoming upset.

"No, he doesn't know. I don't like to tell my family anything. They are so quick to judge."

"So, let me get this straight, you are A'val sister in law? Is Hope your sister?"

"Yes, that's my real blood sister."

"And you don't have anywhere to go?"

"I am homeless, Literally, I been staying in my car. I really need your help. I swear you don't have to worry about nothing. I am a good person, I'm pretty and everything, I just made some really bad choices." she pleaded. "I don't do drugs or steal from people, and I'm sure A'val wouldn't have never told me to call you if I was that kind of person."

Stuff couldn't help but laugh.

"What?" she asked.

"Nothing. You making me feel like I'm a record label owner and you are the Artist and you trying to get me to sign you to my label."

She giggled. "I sound that bad?"

"Horrible."

They both started laughing and soon the operator told her to insert more money.

"What was that?"

"Oh, I'm on a pay phone."

"Wow, so what do you want to do?"

"I want to come with you." she said with confidence." A'val been told me to do this, but I just wasn't ready, but I'm ready if the opportunity still on the table for me."

Stuff was amazed at how blunt she was, "I'mma take you far, far away if you trying to come with me." he told her.

CHAPTER 31

"I don't care," she said.

"Ok, I live in Traverse City, how are you going to get here?"

"The only way I can get there is if you come get me." "Are you serious?"

"Yes. I have nothing and nobody. I'm just being real." she said.

He was quiet for a minute wondering if this was really what he wanted to do. He didn't know Joy but he knew if A'val turned her on to him she had to be a good person. He took a deep swallow and could not believe what he was about to say but he just had to meet her. She sounded way too interesting to him. "Ok, I'll come. This is going to cost you. I haven't been down there in months. This is going to cost you big time." he told her.

She giggled with excitement in her voice. "Thank you so much. You won't regret it." she said. Then she gave him directions to where she would be. Joy hung the phone up and she was happy that she made that call. Although he wasn't interested in her book, she was just happy he was willing to take her in. She knew that when he seen her he would be impressed. She was looking her best today. She packed everything up that she wanted to take with her. She then approached the next couple customers that came to the gas station asking them if they want to buy her car for only $200.00. She was looking so attractive the guys wanted to talk to her and that's how she sold her car, off conversation. The guy that bought it was white and he even gave her his number although she would never call him. After she got her money and signed over the registration, she walked over to the big Super Mart Store to buy hygiene products for herself. After she was done doing a little shopping she waited for hours. It was six hours later and she knew Stuff should have been there. It was only a four-and-a-half-hour trip, so she decided to call him again. He answered and he told her that he was just getting off the freeway.

Minutes later Joy was stepping inside a candy red Mercedes. Stuff was a pretty big guy and he looked funny driving a car although it was a big body car.

"Hi, how are you, I'm Joy again." she said, reaching out her hand.

"Damn, you are beautiful. I'm fine. Am I on Punked or something? Are you sure you homeless?"

She giggled. "No, you are not on Punked. Am I?" she shot back as they drove off.

He laughed. "Hell naw. I'm glad I met you. I need a pretty girl like you on my team. You could really take some of my businesses to a higher level, you know that? Do you know how easy things would be for you, not because you are pretty, but because you are pretty and smart. If you willing to learn, I will teach you a lot."

"I'm ready to learn. I really have to do something with myself."

CHAPTER 32

He looked at her admiring her lips. They were shining with clear lip gloss.

"Anyone ever told you, you looked like that singer girl that dance. I forget her name."

"Ciara?" she said already knowing because she heard it before.

"Yeah! That's her! That's who you favor a lot."

"Thank you" she said as she smiled.

"You welcome, Ok like you were saying. You want to do something with yourself huh?"

"Yes, I was going to college for business but that didn't work out."

"No need for college to run your own business. I can give you a book to read that will tell you exactly what to do. Do you know how much a business book cost compared to a $1,500 class?"

"How much?"

"$16.00."

"Damn for real?" she said.

"Yeah, for real."

"I thought a person needed a degree to run a business."

"Nope that's not true at all. Anything you want to do just as long as it's not a Doctor, Attorney, or something you need a Certificate to do, you don't need college. You can get your knowledge from a book. If you want to run your own daycare, bar, club, fashion line, fragrance, shoe, purse, watch, restaurant, or whatever else. You can buy a book on it and it will show you everything."

"A book will show you all that?"

"Hell yeah. You don't know the power of books, knowledge? Nowadays knowledge is the new money. You better get hip before you get left behind."

"I already feel left behind." she said.

"Let me tell you what my grandfather told me. Although I'm personally mixed with four different nationalities, he was a black man. He told me it used to be a crime for black people to read books or go to school. He even told me that he once heard a quote that said, If you want to hide something from a nigga put it in a book. So, I ask him why is that? You know what he told me?"

"What?"

"He said one day I will find out on my own."

"Did you find out?" she asked.

"I found that it's true because you guys don't like to read and that's where everything is. All the tricks to the trades. I mean you could literally get a book on anything you want to know about. So I make sure I read all the time and that's how I started my businesses."

"Damn, so you are telling me, everything I need is in the books?"

CHAPTER 33

"Yup, everything."

"Yeah, right, that can't be. Where are those books at?"

" I bet you $10,000 to your dollar that if you read one book about how to publish a book you will know exactly what to do. Plus, you will know how to get it into stores."

"Bet, I'm taking that bet."

"Ok as soon as I get home, I'll go on Amazon and find you a book on Publishing and watch what I tell you."

"Ok, I hear you. I just don't believe it's that easy."

"Oh, I never told you nothing was easy," he said.

"It's hard?"

"Not once you know what you are doing. What's hard is sitting and finishing a book."

She giggled, "I like to read."

"Well you will be fine. Trust me, I got you. I'll put you up on a lot of good shit."

"I see. What are you mixed with?"

"I'm black, white, Mexican, and Indian."

"Oh ok. So, what is that word you used over the phone, a fracheee or something."

He laughed. "A franchise?"

"Yes! That word right there!" she said smiling. "What is that?"

"A franchise is when you buy into another company's brand. For example, the popular Burger joints, or taco joints. You can purchase one of them and make money, they already have the system set in place, so basically all you are doing is putting up the money and managing it."

"How much that be costing?"

"It depends, not much though, and you can make good money. You just have to make sure you do your homework on whatever company you want to buy into."

"So which ones you have?"

"I have a few coffee places and I have one burger joint."

"Oh ok, that's cool. That sound pretty good."

"Here, I'll make it sound even better for you. Last year I made over $275,000 off all three and I don't do anything. I have workers that flips the burgers, take orders and all that. I just sit back and collect like a boss. I hire people with degrees, and I don't even have a Diploma or a GED myself. Hell, I dropped out freshman year."

"How is that?" she asked, curious.

"Because I'm the owner. All you need is money to be that. Knowledge to succeed at it." he said smiling.

"Damn, that's what I want to do. I want to have a business but not be there, you know?"

"Of course. Because if you are working at your own business, basically it's your job. A business should run itself no matter if you there or not."

All Joy could think in her head was that he is really smart. She was honored just to be in his presence. "That's weird though, but it makes sense."

"Why weird?"

CHAPTER 34

"I don't know. I was just taught to go to school and get a good job and retire."

"Yeah, that's the poor man mind set. Rich people think opposite then that. They are investors. They invest in Real estate, products that could help people and many other things. See, they do shit you don't get taught in school, they invest."

"Why don't schools teach that? I'm just sitting here thinking and it's like if you don't play sports , there's not nothing you can go to college for and make like ten million a year doing."

"I agree. Now don't get it twisted, if you go to college with an entrepreneur mindset you can take what they teach and use it differently. But even with that said, I rather go buy a book for under twenty dollars just to stay out of debt, you know. Everyone going to school for years and when they get out, they are unemployed, and they owe thousands of dollars."

"Yeah, you're right about that. That's crazy!" she said and then she was silent for a long time. She had to digest everything he had just told her. He was opening her eyes to some new things and no one ever did that for her.

She sat quiet for a while and she couldn't help but think about Daniel while falling to sleep. The man of her life. Daniel stood 6ft2, dark brown skin with a muscular body. The first time he seen Joy talking to a known big time drug dealer by the name of Gator, he wanted to know how close they really were. He had been watching Gator for some months now and he was ready to make his move.

As soon as Joy came out and got into the car with her sister, Daniel followed them. He followed them all the way to a liquor store and as soon as he seen her get out and walk inside, he followed behind her. She was at the counter buying some liquor and when the cashier told her how much, Daniel spoke up.

"Let me take care of that for you gorgeous." He said.

Joy looked up at him right into his eyes and she knew right then in there they were going to be together. This was so her type of guy. Tall, dark, Cocky and confident. She took a deep breath after noting how long she was staring at him. "Thank you, I'm Joy." she said letting him know he had the green light to go further if he chose.

"You welcome, a woman pretty as you don't deserve to pay for nothing." he said. "I'm Daniel." he added shaking her hand firmly.

CHAPTER 35

J oy blushed as she eyeballed his diamond chain. The charm was bigger than her whole hand.

"Joy, it was a pleasure meeting you and I would love to take you out sometime." he said.

Although Joy had a boyfriend at the time, she still agreed. "Sure, take my number," she said. He handed her his phone and she saved her number.

To her surprise, he called her later that night and they went out to dinner.

The second day they went to the movies then out to eat again. Daniel brought her flowers each time and she was loving it. The third day he took her to a huge golf course, and she learned how to golf for the first time. That was the day their first kiss happened. That night when Joy came home, she dumped her boyfriend for no reason at all. She knew that Daniel was the one for her.

A couple weeks later they went out again. This time they flew out to Vegas and had dinner on a rooftop, and later they went back to a 5-star hotel. That was the first night they had sex and fell in love with each other. Daniel had a girl at the time but he left her, got a place with Joy two months later. Although Daniel still had his eyes on Gator he had finally asked Joy if she knew him. She told him they had gone out a few times, but she didn't like him like that. She told Daniel he always called even to this day. Daniel then told her his plan. He was planning to rob him.

Although he was getting money in the streets he explained to Joy how this would take him and her to the next level. He assured her it was safe and all she would have to do was go out a few times with him.

Joy felt safe about the whole thing because the other person in the plan was Daniel. He worked alone when he was about to rob a guy and she liked that. And she also believed that this would be his last time robbing someone. It was, and they both managed to get $90,000 cash and 8 Kilos of Cocaine.

Daniel killed Gator, and Joy to this day had no clue where he put the body because it was never found. After that, Joy and Daniel's relationship took off. They went everywhere and even had sex on more than seven beaches. They got along so good and Joy understood his lifestyle but most of all she trusted him. He bought her anything she wanted and promised her that as long as he was here she would never have to work.

When Joy woke up, she was looking at a big house made out of wood. It was big and unique. She had never seen anything like this before.

"We here, you must have been dreaming because every time I looked at you, you were jumping." Stuff said.

She smiled and raised up to exit the car. "Is this your house?"

CHAPTER 36

"One of them."

"I like this, I've never seen a house like this before in real life."

"Yeah, it's something different." he said.

Joy brought her bag inside and Stuff told her where she could sleep. He had a guest room that looked like the master room. It had a bathroom with a whirlpool, small kitchen, small refrigerator, and a Queen Size Bed that matched the three dressers. Everything was wood.

"This is nice, it's like a little house. No closet?" she asked looking around.

"Yup, right over here." he said as he showed her the closet that was built into the wall. The door was a bookshelf that came open revealing a walk-in closet that was huge."

"Damn, this is nice!" she said, smiling and walking inside the closet. There were mirrors everywhere, plenty of shoe racks, hat racks and plenty of room to put clothes.

"This house came like this or you had this built?"

"I had the whole house built from the ground up. I designed it like this." he said.

She smiled, "Wow, this is really nice. You did a good job."

"Well thank you, come on, let me show you the rest of the house."

He showed her the rest of the house and the best part was his office where he had three big screen computers set up with fax machines, printers and scanners. He had webcams, and many other cameras. Then he had one big printer that set off in the corner.

"I probably can print a book on that big printer huh?" she asked.

"Maybe. You can try. I don't know much about it, but I know all it takes is a quick internet search to find out."

"Yeah, I'll find out." she said, smiling.

Joy was now comfortable and that night her and Stuff had a long talk about business. He told her he was not going to waste any time with her. He was going to bring her to some of his companies tomorrow so she could see how things are being ran. Then he told her will invest in her but first she had to read the two books he gave her.

CHAPTER 37

They were thick but Joy didn't care. One was about business, and the other one was about business on the internet. Joy could not wait to read them. He also told her to take notes and write down everything she felt that was important from each book.

"You have a book about Publishing a Book?" she asked.

"Naw, but we can order one right now." he said, sitting down in front of one of his computers. He searched and about ten popped up. "What about this one? "From prison to the Publishing Game" this book tells you how to write, publish and sell your book, want to check this one out?" he asked.

"Yeah, I'll check it out." she said.

"See the best thing about these kinds of books is if they don't tell you every single thing, usually it will refer you to other books on the same topic."

"Ok, get that one, how much is it?"

"It's only $13.00. You want the E-book or the actual book?"

"Well since I have to read these books just get the actual book, and hopefully when that one come through the mail, I'll be done with these."

Stuff ordered the book for her. He had faith in Joy and he was going to take a chance with her because he saw the hunger in her.

That night, Joy stayed up all night in her own room reading and taking notes. She felt that sleeping would be pointless. She was on a mission and she was going full throttle at it.

It was around 3:30am when Stuff peeked in on her noticing, she was in the computer room. "Damn girl you still up?"

"Yeah, I'm searching for something I had found in the book. I'll be up for the rest of the night for sure."

"Do your thing. I'mma go to sleep, see you tomorrow." he said.

"Did your little hoochie leave yet?"

He laughed, "She just left."

"Oh, she was not cute either." Joy said, with a mug on her face.

Stuff laughed. "Just a piece of meat to me. She not my girl."

"Oh, well if that's what you like."

"Good night, I'm going to sleep."

"Bye," she said, attending back to her computer. "Stuff!" she shouted.

He came right back in. "What's up?"

"Thank you. I really appreciate what you are doing for me."

"Oh, not a problem. This is just the beginning." he told her before closing the door.

Joy was so happy that she had a roof over her head again. Although she was hours away from home, it didn't matter. The only thing on her mind was to get herself together. She had thought back to when she had called Mesha, Armoni and Phia.

"Hello." Mesha answered.

oy was crying so hard she could hardly talk. "Mesha...I need your help!" Joy said in between cries.

"What is it? Are you ok?" Mesha asked.

Mesha, Armoni, and Phia hadn't been talking to her nor going out with her since she had lost her car months ago. They didn't even want to be bothered with her. It took a whole lot to call them, but Joy did it.

"No, I don't have anywhere to go." she said, crying." Can I come stay with you for a little while?"

"Girl you know how Trae is, and plus we are about to fly to the Bahamas for vacation." Mesha said.

"Ok." Joy said, still crying. She hung the phone up and called Armoni. But it was like Mesha had already called Armoni because she had the story and so did Phia. Joy was so mad that she just slammed the phone down.

Joy could not get that thought out of her head. She thought

they were really good friends but when things got rough for her, they didn't want to help nor bother with her.

Thinking about that kept her up longer searching and reading information from the book and the computer. She stopped around 6:00am and went to sleep on the computer. It wasn't long before Stuff had come to wake her up. It was then around 8am. She was wide awake though. She got in the bathtub and got dressed, looking good. Stuff was starting to like seeing her get dressed. She just looked so good to him.

When they finally left, he took her to breakfast at one of his restaurants in Traverse City. Then he took her to the back to show her how everything was running. The next stop was a cell phone store he had set up. He showed her everything about that, even how he made most of his money. She left with knowledge and a new cell phone, so everything was well worth it. He also took her to a hotel he owned. She was impressed because she never knew a person that owned all these things. Stuff was clearly a millionaire, but you would never be able to tell. He had nice cars and houses, but he wasn't too flashy. He even told Joy how much money he brought in off of all his businesses. Stuff had so many investment ventures going on, Joy had lost track.

Around noon they went to lunch at a Coney Island he owned.

"So why Traverse City? You have all this money, why don't you move to Cali or Vegas somewhere?" she asked.

"I like it here. I want to stay close to my businesses, but one day, I'm sure that would be possible but first I want to have a wife by then." he told her.

"How did you get started with all this?"

"I used drug money to start. I did time in prison for a gun, I read a ton of books in my spare time, it was only two years, but it was more than enough for me. When I got out, I said I was going to start investing into legal things, and that's what I did. And you know what I found out?"

"What?"

CHAPTER 39

"I found out that selling drugs was the bottom of the barrel of making money. I didn't see my first million selling drugs. I seen that first million from the shampoo I hit stores with three years ago."

"You have your own shampoo?"

"Yup."

"Shut Up."

"I swear, I'm working on deodorant and body wash also."

"How the hell did you do that?"

"Easy, you can do it too. I'll hook you up with my manufacturer's company. They will come up with a smell for you for just a few hundred dollars. Then the rest is up to you. I'll show you how to distribute through the big stores. I've done commercials and everything. My shampoo is a very big success."

"Wow, that is so crazy! So, you was in the commercials?"

"No, I can be, but I don't like the camera. I would usually hire a model to do that for me or an up and coming Celebrity."

"That's crazy. Why don't A'val have that? That's your boy isn't it?"

"Yeah of course, but A'val don't want to read anything. He doesn't know the power of these books. See when you reading you are discovering new things. I know people that has read one book and it changed their life. A'val has a couple businesses but he could be doing way better but the boy love to sell that weed."

She giggled. "So, do you still sell drugs?"

"Actually, I own a ranch in California. I grow over 5000 pounds a year."

Joy mouth fell open. "What?"

"Yeah, I don't have to touch anything. I'm in the manufacturing business not the distribution business."

Joy was quiet for a few seconds before she said. "So you have all this money and all these businesses. Why don't you have a woman?"

"I did, but she ran out on me with $400,000 cash. She's no longer living, but that was my last relationship which was about a year ago. Since then I just been playing the field waiting until I seen something I wanted."

Joy had stumbled on a real boss. Daniel had nothing on this man when it came to getting money. "Wow, did you have any kids by her?"

"No."

"Do you have kids?"

"I have four, two boys and two girls but they are all staying with their mothers."

"How many different mothers?"

"Just two."

CHAPTER 40

They sat and talked for hours. They had so much in common it was unreal. They were always able to keep a conversation going no matter what the topic was.

A week later, A'val had just picked up seventy-five pounds of weed and was on his way to drop them off when he noticed a police car behind him. "Shiiiit!" he said as he pulled over to the shoulder. He called Hope right away and let her know what was going on. He also told her to get the money out of the house because they were obviously watching him because he didn't believe they had a reason to pull him over. The police slowly walked up to the car while calling for backup. He asked for A'val information, but still wanted to conduct a search because he said he smelled marijuana. A'val stepped out and the officer soon found all the pounds of weed and A'val was arrested and taken to jail. His house was raided as Hope was coming out of it with $40,000 cash. They brought her to jail as well.

Hope was released on a $10,000 bond and A'val had to pay $25,000 cash plus put up one of his houses. He had lost a big chunk of money, but he still was sitting on money to help him make up from the lost.

Hope had become scared and began trying to talk A'val out of selling drugs. She had given him two choices which was to be with her or continue to sell drugs.

A'val had took such a huge loss he wasn't thinking about quitting right now, he was thinking about making his money back. He tried his best to explain how weed wasn't a big deal and he would not get that much time if any, but Hope had made up her mind. She did not want anything to do with him until he was done selling drugs.

Joy and Stuff had heard all about A'val catching a case and they were both surprised. Joy was loving Traverse City. It was peaceful and since she didn't know anyone, no one bothered her.

"Have you talked to A'val?" Joy asked while she was sitting on the couch with a cover over her.

"Yea earlier. He good though. You know your sister tripping though. She don't like that shit." Stuff said as he was in the kitchen pouring Joy and himself some of his famous Kool-Aid.

"She'll be ok. She knew what he did before this happened." Joy said.

"So how did you like that book? From Prison to the Publishing Game?"

"It was good. Very informative, actually it was the shit. Now I know what I'm doing. I'mma need some money from you though." She said with a smile.

"How much?"

"It won't be much, I promise. I'll let you know later though. I should have an estimate."

"Are you sure this going to make you some good money?" he asked.

eah Stuff! This is where it is at, I'm serious. Just trust me on this ok boo?"

"Oh, now I'm boo?" he asked sarcastically.

She just giggled.

Her and Stuff was becoming closer, but she wasn't sexually attracted to him. She had also sensed that he was abusive one day when he had company and was arguing with one of his random girlfriends. She just wanted to be friends with him, but she could tell that he was very attracted to her because he was always trying to flirt. He loved taking her out, but she made sure he knew that she wasn't trying to mislead him in any way.

"You want to go on a lil trip with me?" he asked.

"Where we going?"

"I have to go down to Miami for about a week. You can either stay here, I'll leave you the keys to a car and money or you can come with me."

"I'll stay here. You go ahead and take care of your business. I'll be here when you get back."

"Ok, cool."

"What are you driving?"

"A rental car. I wanted to take one of my trucks, but I'll just rent me something nice."

"Oh lord, what are you going to get?"

"Usually I will rent me a Bentley, but I think I'll rent a Lamborghini for my stay this time."

"That is crazy Stuff. You don't need to rent a Lambo."

He laughed. "It's just for a week. It ain't nothing." he said."

"Ok well have fun. When are you leaving?"

"In about a few hours."

"Why such a short notice?"

"Something came up, I'll tell you later."

"Tell me now so I won't be worried."

"Nothing bad, no need to worry."

"Ok whatever."

"Don't have nobody in my house either." he said before walking to his room.

"What do you mean? You have company, that's not fair Stuff!" she shouted while getting up and following him.

"You don't even know anyone up here. Get a room if it's that serious. Here's enough money to do whatever you want." he said as he threw a knot of money on the bed.

CHAPTER 42

"How much is this?" she asked.

"About five thousand."

"This all for me?"

"Yup, that's all you. I'll put it on your tab." he joked.

She giggled. "Thank you. You did not have to leave this much though. You are too nice.

"You welcome."

Hours later Stuff was gone and Joy was at his house all alone. She soon got herself dressed and decided to go for a drive around town.

When she got inside the Mercedes, the sun was beaming. It was kind of chilly out, but it was a beautiful day. She hopped in and headed straight for the mall.

When she arrived, there was so many people there she couldn't even find a parking spot. She had to park like a half a mile away.

As she walked inside all eyes was on her as if they had never seen a black person before. The place was full of white people and you could count on one hand how many black people was in the whole mall. Joy didn't care, she had money to spend. She went from store to store purchasing everything she wanted. She had so many bags she had to rent a cart. She had been shopping for hours and she was exhausted. Her last store was a Vitamin Store and that's when she seen a familiar face.

"Rino!?" she said with a nod.

He turned around looking like he worked for a law firm. He was dressed in a V-neck sweater that was sky blue. Then he wore some Kaki colored slacks, with some nice dress shoes. He also had some plain glasses on. He was looking like a little nerd, but he was dressed for where he was at. He obviously wanted to blend in. He was like a long lost twin for the rapper Nas, almost identical.

He turned around. "What's up with you? You alright?" he asked with a smile on his face then he gave her a big hug. "What you doing up here?"

"What are you doing up here? That's the question. Then you out here trying to blend in. You from the hood, stop fronting."

They both laughed.

"Shit this how I gotta be. This where I get my money from, so you know I gotta keep the swag together. But for real though, what you doing up here? You looking good too. The last I heard about you was you was homeless, but you in this bitch looking like you eating good to me."

"Homeless?" "Yea,

down bad."

"Who told you I was homeless?"

"Come on Joy, you know I don't pillow talk like that. Just know that's what I heard but clearly that's not true."

"Right, how has Armoni been? Is she here too?"

"Naw she at the crib. I don't take her on my business ventures. She good though, I just bought her a white Corvette, so she all the way good."

Joy shook her head, "You are crazy." she said smiling.

"Have you talked to Daniel?"

"Hell naw! Fuck him!" she spat.

CHAPTER 43

"**D**amn, what happen? Come on, let's go get a bite to eat for we can sit down and talk." he told her.

"I was just speaking. I'll catch you later on."

"How long you gonna be up here?" he asked.

"I live up here now."

"For real?"

"Yeah, I been staying up here for a little while now."

"Man, I be up here bored as hell we need to hit a movie or something tonight."

"Boy please, don't even try it Rino." "What?"

"You know what. Amoni is my friend and I used to mess with Daniel."

"What that mean? He used to cheat on you all the time. Plus, him and Armoni was fucking before me and her hooked up."

"He did not fuck her."

"Yes, he did."

"You are lying."

"I swear on my mom." he said.

"And what you mean Daniel use to cheat all the time?"

"Daniel a playa, you know how that go."

"Yeah maybe we do need to sit down and talk. You done in here?" she asked.

"Yup."

They walked out the store and Rino helped her carry her bags to her car after sitting down for a few hours eating and talking. When they got to the car it was dark but Rino could still see the red paint shining.

"Oh, this how you doing it now?" he asked with a smile.

She smiled. "Yup, go tell them hoes that." she said as she got inside. "Where your car at I'll drive you to it."

"Kool," he said while getting in. "Come on Joy, go to the movies with me tonight, we'll have fun."

"I don't know about that Rino."

CHAPTER 44

"Jy it's me. Come on now. Come hang with me tonight. You know I'm not going to let nothing happen to you. I got you."

She looked at him and noticed his sincere smile. She figured since she wasn't doing anything else, it would not hurt to go out.

"Alright, I will."

"My car right here." he said while pointing to a black Challenger with black tinted windows. "You can hop in with me and leave your car here if you want."

"Ok that's cool. Better yet, I'll park across the street in that other parking lot it says 24 hours. I don't want to get a ticket, everything closed."

"Ok," he said as he got out and followed behind her while she parked.

She then got inside with her purse. She was excited to be out and free. Every time she went out with Stuff it was like he was acting like he was her boyfriend. It felt good to be free to do whatever she wanted.

As they were driving, Armoni called Rino's phone. Before he answered he told Joy to not say anything. She agreed but had an attitude. She let him talk for about ten minutes while sitting in silence listening to her nag. Finally, she squeezed his right thigh.

"Get off." she whispered. He shook his head ok and minutes later he was off.

"Damn, you could have waited." "Oh

really?"

"Naw I'm playing I know that was a little disrespectful, but that's my girl, what you expect? You know how Armoni is," he told her.

"I still can't believe her and Daniel fucked. That is not sitting right with me at all."

"Shit happens, that was before me."

"She should have told me and he should have too."

Rino didn't say anything he just continued to drive while listening to the radio, the latest hit from the rapper Drake. He soon went to a Store and bought a $300 bottle of Champagne. He poured them a cup and they drove a whole hour away to a movie theater.

The movie lasted about an hour and a half before they were on their way back to Traverse City. "So what you have up for tonight?" he asked.

"I'm so tired and my feet hurt so bad from these heels, I think I'mma just lay down and go to sleep. This Champagne got me feeling really good so I know I will sleep good."

"You don't want to come chill with me for a little while?"

"Damn Rino, I been with you all day!" she said, smiling.

"I know, you fun as hell. I don't even know anyone up here. I got a nice hotel room at a resort and I'mma just be chilling tonight."

"Aww, you want me to keep you company?"

"Please, if not, I'll probably go to the Casino again and blow a few thousands."

CHAPTER 45

"**L**ook at you, just throwing money away."

"I got it like that. You need to let me spend some of it on you."

"Feel free. What's the problem?" she asked, taking a sip of her drink.

He laughed. "There is no problem, well we can go shopping tomorrow then."

"That's fine with me, what time do you want me to be ready?"

"Whenever, I already told you I don't know anyone up here."

"Serious Rino? You don't know anyone up here?"

"I mean yeah, but not no females I can chill with. All my white boys up here and they out working right now."

"Ok, I'mma chill with you tonight. I hope you got double beds though. I am not sleeping in the bed with you."

"Why not? I won't touch you."

"That's what they all say."

"I'm not them lame ass niggas you be fucking with."

"You are. Actually, you are lamer. You hated on Daniel earlier and Armoni. That's female shit. I'mma be real with you, you not going to get this ever, but if you want to spend some money on me you can. If that's not fine with you, take me to my car now."

Rino was shocked and silent. He took her straight to her car and dropped her off. He was pissed but he still told her to call him if she wanted to go out again.

Joy got out and she laughed when she got inside the car because she knew that Rino thought he was about to have sex with her. Daniel had taught her well and he had warned her about guys like Rino. She knew he wasn't for the right things. He was a snake and he was willing to do whatever to get in her panties. In fact, too much. Yet they exchanged numbers.

Armoni finally hung her phone up when she heard Joy get out the car. She was pissed and she could not believe Rino or Joy. She then quickly called Mesha and Mesha answered on the first ring.

"Hello."

"Girl, guess what? You not going to believe this."

"What?" Mesha asked knowing it had to be something serious. She could hear it all in her voice.

"Rino was with that bitch Joy up north while he was supposed to be up there taking care of business."

"Whaaat!? You lying!"

"I got some of the conversation recorded on my phone. I am on my way up there right now. He messing with the wrong one!"

"Wait until he come back, don't go way up there with them white folks tripping."

"Fuck that Mesha! I'm legit!"

"I am going with you, come and get me."

"I'm on my way. Pack a light suitcase, we might be up there for a minute."

CHAPTER 46

"That's cool with me, I need a vacation. My man gone for a few days anyways."

"Call Phia and ask her do she want to come too."

"Girl you already know the answer to that. She's coming." Mesha said.

"Well call her for me and tell her to be ready. I'll be over there in thirty minutes." Armoni said before she hung up and began getting herself ready. She packed her a small bag with a couple outfits, and she put her gun in her bag as well just in case.

As she was walking out the house, she called Rino. The first time he didn't answer but the second time he picked up.

"Whats up baby?"

"Nothing, on my way to get some gas." she said.

"Oh ok, where you about to go?" he asked. "Out."

"Out?"

"Yeah."

"Out where and with who?"

"Just me and the girls."

"It's late. Where ya'll going tonight?"

"To many questions Rino. What you been doing?"

"Nothing, chilling."

"I miss you." she said while biting her lip because it hurt to say those words.

"I miss you too."

"Well I was just calling you before I go out."

"Where you going?"

"I think we just about to go downtown Detroit for a couple hours to have a few drinks."

"Oh. Well call me tomorrow, I'm about to crash. I'm tired as hell."

"I bet." she mumbled. "Ok goodnight baby."

"Goodnight."

Armoni hung up and was even more pissed off because Rino didn't tell her he loved her. But minutes later he texted her "I Love You" and that made her smile, but she was still mad and he was in for a big surprise. She headed over to Mesha house and by the time she got there Phia was over there as well.

She blew her horn twice and they came out and got in the car.

"Damn why you driving this car?" Phia asked as she got into the back seat.

It was Armoni's sister new Tahoe. "Girl don't start. I'm not about to drive a flashy ass car up to the boondocks. We will all be in jail." Armoni said.

They all laughed.

After everyone was in, Phia spoke up and said, "I have to go home to get some clothes really quick."

"What you mean? I told ya'll to be ready. Mesha you didn't tell her what I said?"

"Yeah, but the bitch was right down the street when I called her so she just came right over."

"You better hurry up too Phia or I'mma leave you." Armoni said with a serious look on her face.

"Whatever, I won't be long." Phia said.

CHAPTER 47

Armoni arrived at Phia's house and Phia got out and went inside while Armoni and Mesha waited. They waited for fifteen minutes and Phia still wasn't out so Armoni called.

"I'm coming." Phia said when she picked up. "This dude is tripping asking too many questions." she added.

After she said that, Armoni knew it was about to be a problem, so she said. "Ok hurry up girl." Then she hung up. "She in there arguing. He doesn't want her to leave." Armoni said.

Mesha just shook her head and soon Armoni phone rang again. It was Phia.

"What?" Armoni answered.

"Ya'll gone head. Just call me when ya'll get there."

"Why, what happened?"

"Nothing. It's just too late."

"What about your car at Mesha house?"

"Oh, I'll get it tomorrow."

"Alright, I'll talk to you later." Armoni said before she hung up. "She on lock, she in for the night."

Mesha started laughing. "Oh, this is what I wanted to ask you. Did Rino take her up there with him?"

"No I don't think so. I think they just ran into each other up there, because I remember him dropping her off to her car plus he was asking her to spend a night with him. So she must of already been up there. I don't really know but I'm going to find out, I bet you that." Armoni said.

Joy drove off and went to the nearest gas station to get some gas. It was almost twelve and she was ready to lay down and relax. She went inside and paid thirty dollars for some gas then came back out and began pumping it.

As she was standing there, there was a guy across from her pumping gas also and he was staring at her. She was never into white guys but this one looked cute to her and he had a little swag about himself. He was driving a nice jaguar.

Finally, he spoked to her. "How are you? Are you from around here?" he asked.

"I'm fine. No, I'm not from here," she said.

"I knew it when I saw you. You are so fine, are you single?" he asked which shocked her because he was so outspoken and confident.

She smiled. "Yes, I'm single and thank you. You're a cutie as well."

He then began walking over towards her. He was dressed nice

wearing blue designer jeans with the matching shirt. Plus he was wearing the hat to match.

"I'm Chase." he said as he extended his hand.

She shook it with a smile. "I'm Joy, nice to meet you."

"Same here, wow, you have a pretty smile."

"Thank you."

"Your welcome. How long are you in town?"

"For a while."

CHAPTER 48

 "**Y**ou have to let me take you out. Trust me, you not about to meet no one up here that's going to catch your eye, far as dudes go."

She giggled. "Oh really? So, what's that supposed to mean?"

"It means, give me a chance." he said waiting on a response.

"I don't know."

"Just hang out with me one time. If you don't enjoy yourself, you won't have to ever worry about me again." he said looking in her eyes.

"Ok, you can take me out Chase."

"Ok good, you have a number?"

She gave him her number and finished pumping her gas. Chase was a surprise for her and she liked his confidence. Although he sounded like he could be a black dude you can tell he just grew up that way. It was just him. He wasn't trying to be something he really wasn't.

Joy finally arrived home and soaked in a steaming tub of water with bubbles. She stayed in there for nearly an hour just thinking about everything she's been through. She felt so blessed to be back in a great position.

As she was stepping out, she noticed Stuff calling. She answered and he was just checking on her making sure things was fine. She told him all that she did, and they said their goodbyes. As soon as she hung up her phone, rang again. As she looked at the area code, she knew it was from someone up there and the only person that had her number was Chase. She smiled as she answered. "Hello."

"Hello, is this Joy?"

"Yes, this is she."

"You're not sleeping, are you?"

"No, not yet, I'm on my way though. Is this Chase?"

"Yup, I liked that you remembered my name."

"I'm good with names."

"Damn, you just going to rain on my parade like that?"

She giggled. "Sorry! I was just saying."

"So, what are you doing here in Traverse City?"

"It's a long story."

"Well I want to hear it. Or would you rather tell me tomorrow while we at dinner?"

She giggled. "You think your slick, don't you?"

"Naw, Naw I'm really just asking."

"Sure Chase, we can do dinner tomorrow."

"Ok cool. Well I'mma let you get that beauty sleep and I'll get me some sleep too. I'll call you tomorrow around five, is that cool?"

"That's perfect." she said. She then hung up shaking her head. So far, she liked Chase.

The next morning Joy was up early and out driving to get herself some breakfast. Before she picked a restaurant, she called Rino.

"Hello."

"Are you sleep?" she asked noticing his voice.

"Yeah. What time is it?" he asked.

"7am, get up. I need your help."

"Who is this?"

"This Joy, retart!"

"Oh, what's up?"

CHAPTER 49

"**I** need you to tell me where I can get some good pancakes at."

"Umm hold on." he said as he got himself up." Meet me where your car was at last night. I'll go with you. I'm starving."

Joy took a deep breath regretting that she wasted her time calling him.

She didn't expect for him to want to go. "Alright. I'll be there in about fifteen minutes."

"Ok, I'll be there." he said before hanging up.

Joy continue to drive. She loved the scenery in Traverse City. The street she was on was like a strip. There were at least fifty different hotels on this street. Every restaurant was on it also. There was also a beach. The whole place looked alive.

Finally, she arrived to meet Rino. As soon as she drove in the parking lot, she noticed his car. She then called him as she was parking.

"You can just ride with me." he said, as soon as he answered.

"Ok, here I come."

CHAPTER 50

A rmoni and Mesha had followed Rino to meet Joy and they were now staking out across the street from them in the mall parking lot.

"Look, is that her?" Armoni asked.

"Yup, that's her. Damn she got her a nice Benz. I wonder how she do that." Mesha asked.

"Fuck her. She is messing with my man."

"So, what are going to do?"

"We going to wait. I want to see where they go."

"Oh my god. Why don't you just drive over there, block them in and fight her?"

"Naw, I'm not trying to go to jail. Just chill. Let me handle this."

"You want to play the spy game and shit, we going to be up here forever."

"I told you before you left, I was going to be up here for a minute. I don't want to hear that shit Mesha, I told you at the beginning."

Mesha was silent because Armoni was right, she did tell her to pack a bag so there was nothing she could do.

Soon they were on the move. They followed them to a restaurant where they both went in and set down to eat.

"Look at this shit. I can't believe this." Armoni said as she parked at a hotel across the street.

"I don't see how you can sit and watch another female be with your man. I would have been in there getting my man and she would have been picking her teeth up off the floor." Mesha said.

Armoni just turned and looked at her." And that's why you have a record. Being stupid. I want to fuck both of them up, but I want to see what's what."

"You already see what's what. They are fucking! What more do you want?"

"Mesha please shut up talking to me."

They sat there a whole hour then they followed them back to Joy's car where he dropped her off and they went their separate ways. For a second Armoni wanted to follow Joy but she wanted to keep tabs on Rino because she knew he was trying to fuck Joy. Although she turned him down the first night, things could change.

 ou should have followed her ass to see where she was going." Mesha said.

"No, she is not my concern. I'm up here for Rino. I'm trying to see what his sneaky ass doing."

"You see what he's doing. He's cheating!"

"Whatever Mesha. They didn't even do anything. I want to catch a bitch up at his room. I'll deal with him about the Joy situation but while I'm all the way here I want to kill two birds with one stone. Although it may hurt me a little watching all this shit, I'll be alright."

Hours later Joy was on her way to dinner with Chase. She was excited and she was hoping that everything went smooth. She hadn't had sex in so long and she was becoming sexually frustrated. She was trying to wait to meet someone that was worth giving it to but tonight if Chase make the right moves, she was going to have sex with him. Although she was horny when she was with Rino last night, she wasn't going to have sex with Rino no matter what he did or was willing to do. She was turned off by how he was telling on Daniel. That just wasn't cool in her eyes and she had lost a little respect for him for that. Joy believed every man should be so confident in himself that he would never have to hate on another guy to get what he wanted. She knew he wanted to have sex with her, but he blew it bigtime that night.

Right when she arrived to hop in the car with Chase, she received a text message from Rino. *"Sorry about last night. I know I acted like a sucka by hating on Daniel. I normally don't do shit like that, but I wanted you so bad I didn't really know how to come at you. I noticed you had changed your attitude towards me, and I want to apologize. You are so sexy though Joy. I'mma just be real with you. Hope you forgive me. I know you probably on the date you was telling me about, so have a good time."*

Joy laughed to herself as she was impressed how he read her mind. She instantly forgave him and respected him for being honest and upfront. She exited her car and got in with Chase.

"Hey beautiful. You are looking slamming!"

She smiled. "Thank you, so are you."

"Well I try." he said as he drove off and headed to a fancy restaurant. They set down and ate and talked about everything then left and Chase took her back to her car. He was trying to be a gentleman and not make her think that he just wanted to just have sex with her.

Joy was a little upset because she was hoping he asked her to hang out for a little longer. But they just said their goodbyes and departed.

CHAPTER 52

Joy went home and started reading her book. She knew she had to at least start looking for an Editor, and a Graphic Designer so she could have a cover. She fell to sleep thinking about everything she was going to do in the morning and hours later her alarm clock was going off. She got up, took a shower and got dressed. She then called a number to an Editor she had found in Traverse City on the internet after doing a quick Google search. She called him around 10am and he told her to meet him at his office. She used the navigation inside the car to find where she was going, and she quickly realized that his office was his house. It was a nice tan colored home with a two-car garage on each side of the house. It was unique because the both driveways met in the middle and connected to one another.

She called him as soon as she put her car in park and he told her to come in. She got all her papers together and walked up to the door.

"Hi Joy, how are you? I'm Darl." he said with a pleasant smile while reaching to give her a handshake.

"Hello, nice to meet you."

"So, what do we have here?" he asked as he took what she had in her hands and led her to a huge room where a big desk was, a computer, couch, chairs and a whole lot of Art Pictures.

"This is so nice. Do you draw?" she asked.

"Yes, I'm an Artist as well."

"This is a very nice house. It seems like it's bigger on the inside." she said.

"Thank you. Have a seat. Make yourself comfortable. Before we start the editing process, I just have a few questions I want to ask you first."

"Ok."

Darl was 35 years old which surprised Joy when she had talked to him on the phone. For some reason she had thought that she was going to be dealing with an old person, but she was wrong. Darl was still young and very comfortable to be around.

They met for two hours talking about Joy's book then started getting a little personal.

"What inspired you to write this book?" he asked.

"At the time I was going through something and I had a lot inside of me that I needed to get out and the only way I knew to get it out was on paper."

"That's interesting." he said, while shaking his head up and down.

"Do you live in this big old house by yourself?" she asked.

CHAPTER 53

He smiled, "Unfortunately yes...Well you do know that you will have to get your book typed on a computer before I start the editing process right?"

"Oh really? Ok I can do that, What else?"

"I also can typeset your book. Which is putting your book in book form. Are you familiar with that?"

"A little."

"Well I'm assuming that you are a Self-Publisher?"

"Yes."

"Ok, well I do Editing. I typeset, and I can do covers. I'm your one stop shop, I can help you get your book all the way together for a good price if you're up for it."

She smiled. "Yes! Of course. I would love for you to help me out."

"I do it all and I do it well." he said with a smile.

"So how much is all of this going to cost me?" she asked.

"Well since you are a very attractive woman, let me see." he said as he got a pencil and a piece of paper. "It usually cost about $200 for typesetting but I'll charge you half of that which is only $100."

"Thank you." she said smiling. She was loving being around white people. They were super nice and they were always willing to give first before anything.

"Editing? Depending on how many words you have all together."

"Well I counted the words on a few of my pages, would that help?" she asked.

"Yes of course."

"Ok I counted about 403 and like 423 on another."

"Ok, how many pages is it total? Are they numbered?"

"Yes, the number is on the bottom right."

"Ok, you have 198 pages you have wrote. Now let's multiply that number by 400, which gives us a total of a number between 70,000 words and 80,000 words."

"Is that a lot?"

"Yeah, that's pretty long."

"How long do a book have to be?"

"There's no requirements. A book can be 50 pages. No one has a say so in that, but the Author. Unless you have a publisher. Some publishers require you to have a certain amount of words."

"Oh ok. I didn't know that."

"Ok so to edit, let's say 75,000 words, I'm just going to charge you one thousand flat on that. Editing is expensive and usually I would be charging over a thousand for sure."

CHAPTER 54

Joy looked surprised and she was so thankful that he was giving her deals on everything.

"A good cover usually cost about $500 to $2000. I'll do a great job for you and only charge you $300. So, you will owe me about $1400 for everything. Is that Ok?"

"Yes! Yes!" she said smiling.

"I can also help you shop your book around into stores and to agents, but we'll talk about that later."

"Ok, thank you Darl so much! You really don't know how much I appreciate this."

"I'm glad I can help you Joy."

By the time Joy was leaving Rino was calling her. "Hello."

"What's up Almond Joy?" He said trying to be funny.

She giggled. "Real cute. What's going on?" she asked while getting into the car.

"Nothing chilling. What you eat today?"

"Actually, I haven't ate, I'm starving."

"What you want to eat? Let's meet up?"

"Ok, But I don't know what I want."

"The resort I'm staying at is right off a beach and they have some good food. They will cook you steak, shrimp, or even pizza." he said.

She giggled, "You had me when you said shrimp. I love shrimp. That will work for me right now."

"Ok, come through."

"Just tell me where your hotel at. If it's near the beach, I'm sure I can find that." she said. He gave her directions and she headed over.

Armoni and Mesha was sitting in the parking lot of Rino's Hotel and they had been there for hours now. Armoni was waiting on him to bring a female back, but it never happened.

"You just need to go snap on him as soon as you see him. You have enough dirt on him. Him messing with Joy is bad enough." Mesha said.

"No, I need to catch him in the act."

"Armoni, we will be up here for years. You see the boy not bringing females to where he lay his head at, that's a rule girl."

Armoni was silent thinking about what Mesha was saying. She was getting tired of staking out on him while calling him acting like she was at home.

"So, what do you think I should do miss know it all?" Armoni asked.

"You want me to tell you what I would do or what I think you should do?"

Armoni shook her head, "Stop playing Mesha." "Ok,

I think-."

"Wait, wait, wait." Armoni said as she cut Mesha off when she seen Rino driving up. Joy was right behind him in the same red car they had seen her in before. "Look at this shit here." Armoni said.

"What?" Mesha asked, trying to see what Armoni was seeing.

"Look, there go Joy and Rino ass right over there."

"Oouu."

CHAPTER 55

 "Yeah. I told you. All I had do was be patient. I knew he would slip.

"I feel like killing both of them." Armoni said.

Mesha looked at her wondering whether she was serious or not and by the look on her face she was dead serious. Armoni let them both walk inside, and she was just plotting on her next move. She had already known his room number. She had got that when she followed him inside yesterday. They sat and waited for about ten minutes before Armoni had made up her mind.

Joy was sitting on the bed looking around the room and out the patio where there was a plain view of the beach. Rino was walking around with his shirt off while sipping on a bottle of wine. They had already ordered the food and were just waiting on it.

"What you been up too?" he asked.

"Well right now, I'm working on this new book. I'm trying to publish my own book."

"What kind of book?"

"A hood story."

"Oh ok, is there a lot of money in that?"

"Yeah, you can make good money. I'm new to the industry but we will know in a few weeks if there is good money in it or not," she told him.

"Well if I can help you in anyway let me know, you know I got homeboys that own record shops and little bookstores, so when it come out, I'll get you into their stores as a start, you know."

"Yeah, that sounds good. I'll keep that in mind." "So what--."

He stopped as he heard a knock at the door. "Damn that was quick as hell."

"That's the food?" she asked.

"Got to be," he said as he walked to the door and opened it up without asking who it was. As soon as he opened the door his eyes grew big and Armoni sprayed mace into his eyes, face, nose and mouth.

"Ahhh shiiiit! Chill!" He shouted as Armoni and Mesha rushed through the door heading for Joy.

Armoni got to Joy first as she was trying to get off the bed. "You fucking my man bitch!" she yelled while grabbing her hair and yanking her to the floor.

CHAPTER 56

While Rino was in the bathroom trying to wash all the mace from his eyes, Mesha and Armoni was slinging Joy all over the room. Joy was fighting back, but there wasn't much she could do. There were blows after blows coming her way until Armoni pulled out her gun.

She aimed it at Rino as he was coming from the bathroom. "You fucking this bitch?!" she asked.

Everything stopped and the whole room was in slow motion. Mesha stopped fighting and so did Joy. Everyone was still.

"Baby calm down."

"Don't baby me!"

Rino had his hands up with his shirt still off. "It's not what it looks like. We didn't do nothing." he said with his hands up. "I swear we didn't do nothing. Put that gun down. What are you doing?" he asked.

"Fuck you Rino! I heard the conversation! She's fun huh? You want to spend some money on her huh? You want to sleep in the bed with her huh? Then you told the bitch I fucked Daniel. That's not even true. Why would you lie to try to fuck my so called friend!"

Rino was lost for words and he was wondering how she knew what she knew. He was praying Armoni don't pull the trigger.

"Baby you are tripping. Look, they either going to call up here in a second or send someone up here to see what's going on."

"And that's when you are going to tell them that everything is ok." she told him. And seconds later, they heard a knock at the door.

"Answer it." she told him.

He did.

"Is everything ok? There were loud noises coming from one of these two rooms. Your neighbors said they heard it as well, so it didn't come from them."

Rino put up a fake smile. "Yeah I was wrestling with my girlfriend and we kind of knock something over but everything is ok."

"You sure?" the short white guy asked while looking into Rino eyes.

"Yes sir."

"Ok. Well you know if it happens again, I'm going to send the police up here."

"Oh no need for that. Everything is fine."

"Okie-dokie," he said before he walked away.

Rino shut the door. "See you tripping. You know how much shit I have in here? You about to get all of us arrested.

"I don't care." Armoni said, still pointing the gun at him. She soon lowered it and pointed at his private area. "I should shoot you right in the dick since you can't control it."

CHAPTER 57

"**A**rmoni, come on, relax with that gun. He's not worth going to jail for." Mesha said. She had never seen Armoni act like this. She knew she had to be very pissed.

"He is worth it. He's well worth it Mesha. Matter fact, he is so worth it that-"

Boom!

The loud shot rang out through the whole hotel and Rino dropped to the floor screaming and holding his private area. It was so loud you could not tell where it came from. She had shot him.

"Oh my god!" she said dropping the gun on the floor and backing up with her hand over her mouth.

"We got to get out of here, come on!" Mesha said as she picked Armoni up off the floor and ran out the door.

Joy stood there. She was shocked. She couldn't believe Armoni pulled the trigger. Although she didn't mean it, it was still shocking. Joy didn't know what to do. Rino was screaming in pain.

"Close the damn door!" he said, and Joy ran quickly as instructed.

Armoni and Mesha was on the elevator going down while Armoni was crying none stop. "I killed him! I didn't mean too, Mesha!"

"Shut up! Pull yourself together right now before this elevator stops. We are going to walk right out of here without anyone asking us any questions, but you have to look normal." Mesha said as she was whipping the tears from Armoni's face.

"I'm going to jail." she cried.

"No you're not. Pull yourself together." Mesha said as she smacked her in the face to snap her out whatever mode she was in.

Soon the elevator opened and Armoni face was swollen from crying but she had cleaned up the best she could.

"Did you hear that big bang?" An old lady asked.

"Yes, is it raining out?" Mesha said as she continued to walk.

The service desk was confused, and they had no clue where the bang came from.

They gave every room a call to make sure things was ok, but the same white guy that had knocked on Rino door was suspicious. He headed up to Rino's room.

Joy had already gone next door to the neighbors to pay them to keep their mouth closed. Rino gave her seven thousand to give to them and he made Joy put him in the bed and cover him up.

"What they say?" Rino said still in pain while breathing hard. "Shhiiiit!."

CHAPTER 58

"They won't say anything, but we have to get you to a hospital." she said, and they soon heard a knock.

Joy was scared and she didn't know what to do. She was moving as fast as she could. She even threw some water on her face. By the time she opened the door she only had a shirt covering her breast.

Her hair was all over the place from Armoni trying to pull it out, but it look like she was having rough sex.

When the guy seen her, he was speechless to be seeing a nice shaved pussy in front of his face. She did that just to tease him a little. "Umm. Did you hear a noise?" he asked.

"Yes, a big boom noise." she said as she put the shirt over her vagina, revealing her breast. " Oh my, I'm sorry." she said smiling.

"Nooo, I'm sorry to interrupt! I'll go." he said turning red in the face and turning his head to walk away. He glanced one more time before he took off walking. Although he noticed the scratches on her face, he left it alone.

Joy just smiled and closed the door.

"What happen?"

"We good. We have to get you out of here. She shot you in your dick?"

"I will be in way more pain than this. Naw, right by it though." he said taking deep breathes. "This shit is on fire, shit!"

Armoni and Mesha made it to the car no problem and Mesha was driving. She drove out of there nice and smooth and they were almost out of the hot zone. Armoni was still crying and fanning herself.

"I didn't mean to shoot him," she cried.

"I know, calm down until we get out of here."

"I didn't mean too, I swear. I just wanted him to-"

"Shhh! Relax, we going to be alright just relax." Mesha said as she was trying to find her way around. "You didn't kill him, he's ok. He deserves that one shot. He'll survive." Mesha said as she looked at Armoni and smiled.

Armoni looked around and couldn't figure out why she was smiling. She was still nervous and shaking.

"Look you have to get all this dope out of here before you call the police." he said in severe pain. He told her when everything was packed up to walked out with it on her back while holding a throw away minute phone he gave her. As soon as she got to her car and put everything in the trunk, she dialed 911 and told them someone had been shot. She then slammed the phone on the ground, breaking it into pieces. She then sped off and headed home without stopping anywhere extra.

As soon as she got home, she could not stop walking around. She was furious that they had jumped her for no apparent reason, and she could not wait to see them again. Her mind was racing a million miles per hour and she knew she had to do something to calm herself down, so she went and sat in the Jacuzzi.

bout thirty minutes in, she got a call from Chase. "Hello."

"Hey beautiful."

"Hi Chase."

He could hear in her tone that something wasn't right with her. "What's wrong? Are you ok?"

"Not really."

"Why? What happened?" he asked, sounding like he really wanted to know.

Before she began to talk, she started crying. "Hold on." she said as she set the phone down to get her cry out.

About five minutes later she picked it back up and Chase was still on there waiting. "Hello. I'm sorry."

"It's ok, don't worry about it. What happened?" he asked.

"I got into a fight with a friend."

"A fight? With a friend? A girl or guy?"

"A girl, well two girls."

"Why were you guys fighting?"

"She thinks I was messing around with her man."

"Were you?"

"No! not at all. We were just friends. He might have wanted more but he wasn't going to get it."

"Who jumped you?"

"Two of my old friends. Look Chase I don't really want to talk about this. I just want to relax."

"I'm sorry. Well can I at least keep you company? I promise to not get on your nerves. I'll get us a nice room, get you a massage and everything. I know you don't want to be alone."

She smiled and shook her head. Chase was always trying no matter what the situation was. "Ok Chase, but let me warn you, my face a little messed up."

"I don't care about that. I just want to be in your company."

When they hung up, Joy got herself dressed and went to go meet up with Chase.

It was getting dark and Joy couldn't wait to get that massage he promised her.

Armoni tried calling Rino twenty times, but she got no answer. "He's dead Mesha." she said, getting ready to shed tears.

"No he's not. He'll be ok. He's probably at the hospital."

"I want to go back."

"Armoni, what is wrong with you? You just shot him and now you want to go back?"

"I have to. Turn around."

"Hell no, you are really tripping over this nigga. This not funny Armoni."

"Turn around." she said again calmly.

"Are you serious? We are almost home, what the hell?"

"Turn around! Damn Mesha, turn the fucking car around!" she shouted as she grabbed the steering wheel and that's when the whole car begins flipping sideways on the highway. It flipped at least seven times and they landed inside a ditch upside down.

CHAPTER 60

There was glass everywhere and no one was moving. Cars stopped and people got out to help. Armoni and Mesha was leaking blood from several different places. They both was knocked out and no one knew if they were dead or alive.

Later that night Joy and Chase was lying in bed together right after she had just finished getting a massage.

"Thank you, I feel so much better now."

"You're welcome. That's what I'm here for."

"You are such a sweetheart. Why can't all men be nice like you?"

"All men not Chase." he said, smiling.

"You're silly. Is there anymore chicken left? I haven't eaten all day."

"I knew you were hungry. Trying to act like you wasn't."

"I really wasn't at first. I wasn't thinking about eating until I got that massage."

Chase laughed while setting up and fixing her some of the chicken he was eating. "I really like you Joy." he said as he handed her a plate full of chicken.

"That's so sweet. I really like you also."

"Do you think I have a chance of being with you in the future."

"Chase. You haven't told me what you do yet, for a living."

"I did, I told you I have rich parents."

"What else you do though?"

"Ok I sell a little drugs."

"What kind of drugs Chase?"

He shook his head and said, "Weed, Cocaine, and Pills."

"See I knew it. Do you plan on stopping anytime soon?"

"Umm, it depends."

"Depends on what?"

"Depend on if I can have you or not. I would stop for you. I will go back to work to be with you," he said.

She smiled. "You are too sweet." she said as she bit into her chicken.

CHAPTER 61

L ater that night around 1am they had both dozed off to sleep and Joy was lying on his chest. Chase eased up to go to the bathroom and it woke her up.

"What time is it?"

"1 o clock."

"Where you going?"

"To the bathroom."

"Oh," she said as she got up too and while he was in the bathroom she stripped down to her underwear and got underneath the covers.

When Chase came out, he seen her clothes on the floor. He didn't see any panties or a bra, so he knew that she wasn't butt naked. "Getting comfortable?"

She smiled. "Yes, I can't sleep in clothes."

He stripped all his clothes off down to a white tank top and basketball shorts then slid underneath the covers with her and they begin to cuddle.

"You tired?" he asked, he was holding her trying to spark a conversation.

"A little. Are you?"

"Not really." "What's

wrong?"

"Nothing. I'm just happy to be next to you."

"Aww your sweet." she said kissing him on his nose.

"Thanks, I feel a little special," he said.

"What? That wasn't good enough for you?" "I

didn't say that. I just said thanks."

"Whatever, you want a kiss on the lips?" she asked. She knew he wasn't going to ask himself, so she did.

"Why not?" he said moving in for a kiss. Once they locked lips they were stuck. They tongue kissed and Chase was feeling all over her body. She had thought he was shy, but he was proving her wrong. Chase begin kissing her neck slowly making his way down to her belly button. He kissed all around it and ran his warm, wet tongue in circles, working his way to her sensitive spot, right on her waistline. He notice her body responding and jerking so he pulled the covers back even more and started working his way down even more, now kissing her thighs.

Joy was relaxed and was feeling so good. She was hoping that he didn't stop because he was doing a good job making her whole body catch chills.

Soon she felt her panties sliding off and when she looked down, he was pulling them off with his mouth. He slid them all the way off then slowly kissed his way back up her legs until he got between her thighs.

CHAPTER 62

Joy was rubbing her titties as she felt Chase licking and sucking her pussy softly. She put her hand on his head and mashed his face into her deeper and that's when she felt his tongue inside her. "Oooh Chase, don't stop! Right there," she whispered.

He continued to eat her out until her whole body was shaking beyond her control. He continued although she was shaking and cumming, wanting to make her cum a second time. This time he stuck two fingers inside her while he was licking and sucking on her clit.

"Shhhhit!" she moaned with her back arched and her head nearly hanging off the bed. "Awhhhh!" she shouted. "Chaasse!" she shouted. "Don't stop!"

He made her cum once again and then she collapsed and told him to wait. She could not believe he wasn't trying to have sex with her. He just wanted to eat her pussy. And since she had cum twice already, she was out of commission and all she wanted to do is go to sleep.

Chase didn't seem to mind that she had told him to hold on. He just went washed all her juices off his face and came back to hold her again. Joy was snoring within minutes.

They fell asleep and didn't wake up until nine the next morning. Chase was up first, and he had ordered them both breakfast. When the breakfast arrived, he woke her up.

"I can get used to this," she said with a smile. "Breakfast in bed."

"That's no problem. I can do this for you every morning."

"You know how to cook?"

"No, But I'll have a cook if I have to or I'll go out every morning to your favorite restaurant."

She smiled. "You are too nice Chase."

"Is that bad?"

"No not at all. I love a man that's nice to me."

"Oh, ok just checking."

"No, your fine," she said thinking about last night. Chase had made her feel good and he didn't ask for anything in return. Joy was so used to dealing with guys that always wanted something in return for what they did especially when it came down to oral sex.

"I'm going to go jump in the shower," he told her.

"Ok." she said as she picked up her cellphone to call Stuff. She was wondering why he hadn't called her. She also thought about Rino and how he was doing. She was hoping that he had made it to the hospital before he lost too much blood.

She didn't get an answer from Stuff so she sent him a text message and he called her back within three minutes.

"Hey!" she answered.

"Joy, what's up?"

"Nothing, eating some pancakes, what are you doing?"

He laughed. "You love you some pancakes. I'm not doing anything. I'm getting ready to go eat myself."

"You been having some fun?"

"Somewhat. I kind of miss you though."

"You do?"

eah, I wish you would have come with me. You could have had you some fun."

"Maybe next time."

"Did you take care of your book stuff?"

"Yeah, I actually found an editor right here in Traverse City."

"Really?"

"Yup. So, he's helping me right now."

"That's good. Let me know if you need any more money. I don't know how much it cost to get a book published the way you are going about it."

"What you mean, the way I'm going about it?"

"You know, the way I know is to submit your book to a big publisher and if they want to sign you, they sign you and they give you a big advance. You don't have to pay for nothing."

"Oh, naw I'm going to self-publish my book and sell it myself and make them big publishers come to me."

"I like that. That's smart. Did you finish that book, From Prison to the Publishing Game?"

"I finished that before you left. You don't even remember. Let me find out you don't be listening to me."

He laughed. "Naw, I listen I just forgot. Sorry about that. Well I'll see you in a couple of days. I'll call you later, I have to order this food, the lady just came to my table."

"Ok, talk to you later," she said. She hung up the phone and A'val was calling minutes later.

"Hello."

"What up? You awake?"

"Yeah."

"I know you heard what happened."

"No, what?"

"Armoni and Mesha got into a bad car accident and they both are in intensive care."

"What?"

"Yeah, the car flipped over multiple times."

"What? Where?"

"They were like in the Saginaw area."

"How did it happen?"

"They don't know yet. They car was the only one involved."

"Damn," she said, dropping her fork not able to eat anymore. "That's crazy."

"Yeah I know. Hope just went up to the hospital to bring them flowers."

Joy was speechless. She was wondering how that could have happened. She had no clue.

"Well I was just calling you to tell you that. You still up north with Stuff?"

"Yes."

"How is that working out for you?"

"Good. Really good thank you."

"No big deal."

"How is your case going?"

"So far they offered me a year, I might take it and just get work release."

CHAPTER 64

"Oh, that's not bad at all."

"Nope not at all."

"How are you and Hope?"

"We ok, we good."

"You sure? You didn't sound too sure."

"Oh naw, I'm driving. We're good though."

"Ok, well call me if you find out anything else that happened about the accident."

"Ok I got you."

Joy hung up and shook her head. Now she wanted to get in touch with Rino to see if he was ok. She already knew he had heard about what happen. But she still wanted to check on him and make sure he was ok.

"Hey, where is the nearest hospital around here?" she asked when she seen Chase coming out the bathroom. He told her and she was going to go up there and visit Rino when she left Chase. Chase didn't ask why, and she was glad that he didn't.

Later on that day after she had left Chase, she was up at the hospital visiting Rino. She had no trouble finding him. Although she didn't know his whole name, he was one of three black people in the hospital. She sat and talked with him for nearly an hour and he told her who to call and give the drugs to that she left with. He told her he would probably have to stay in there for another week. He had also heard about Armoni and Mesha. He had been praying for them both and as soon as he got well he was going straight home. The police had been up there to question him so he told her to be careful when she left because he was almost sure that the police were watching him and whoever came to see him.

Before Joy left, she kissed him on the forehead and told him she was sorry for what happened. Then she left heading straight for her editor Darl house. She stayed over there until it was dark out and Chase was calling non-stop, but she didn't answer because she was busy. She was going to call him later.

When she left Darl's house she went and did what Rino wanted her to do. She dropped all the dope off to some white boys Rino knew. She then called Chase as she was on her way back home.

"I called you like fifteen times." Chase said when he first answered the phone.

She giggled. "I'm sorry, I was busy working on my book."

"Oh, what are you doing tonight? Can we hang out?"

"Mmm. I will love too, but I have to go home and proofread this book."

"You can proofread with me. I won't bother you."

She giggled. "I'll see tomorrow. We might hang out tomorrow ok."

"Alright then, I see how it is."

"Don't be like that Chase." she said.

"I'm not. I'm fine. I'll catch you tomorrow."

CHAPTER 65

O ne month later

Joy and Stuff were on their way to a printing shop located right outside of Traverse City. She had received a proof copy of her book some days ago and she almost passed out. She was so shocked and happy about her accomplishment.

She cried and hugged Stuff about twenty times that day. Joy had ordered 1000 copies of her book and she had just received a call letting her know that they were ready to be picked up or shipped.

"Are you excited?" Stuff asked while driving. "Yes!

Very excited! It seemed like it took forever!"

"No, it only took you a couple months. That's not long at all."

"Right. But when you don't have things of your own, everyday counts. You been taking care of me since I've been up here, the beginning of summer. I owe you so much." she said.

"No, not at all. I just want to see you doing good. You deserve it."

Soon they were putting boxes inside the trunk and into the back seat.

"Just take me to Pontiac. I know my city going to show me mad love!" she said with a big smile on her face.

"How about I get you a rental car and you drive yourself down there and see what happens."

"Ok, cool."

"Meanwhile, leave me with like a hundred books, I'll put some in my store and--"

CHAPTER 66

"I have a list of bookstores I'll give you and you can just mail copies to them with all my information. If they review the book and like it, they will order in bulk from us."

"Ok. Whatever you need me to do, let me know. I have some guys I'll call up as well. We going to make this happen, don't worry."

Joy arrived in Pontiac at around 4pm. The sun was shining and all she had to do was find where she wanted to start. She called a few people she knew, and they were happy to purchase a book from her for fifteen dollars.

Soon she arrived at a gas station that was located on a street called Perry. She parked in the parking lot and began trying to sell her book.

"Hi, come here for a minute." she said to a young guy.

"What's up baby?"

"This is my book, Turning Tables, it's about a girl that had hit rock bottom after her boyfriend was indicted. But she bounced back by robbing a drug dealer she was sleeping with. She moves to Vegas and starts a new life but the guy she robbed is after her. Trust me it's really good, can you please support it. It's only fifteen dollars," she said.

"Fifteen?" he asked as he went into his pocket and gave her twenty. "Keep the change."

"Thank you so much. Can I get a picture with you holding my book? I want to put it on my Facebook page," she said.

"Yeah that's cool. I'll take a picture with you."

Joy asked a girl to take a picture of them two and she sold her a book as well, then had the guy take a picture of them. Joy stayed up there for hours and people was showing her a lot of love. Some sales she didn't get but she didn't worry about rejection. That was just fuel to her fire. That was all part of the game. She knew that it would be people saying nasty things to her and it would be people supporting her.

That whole day, she had sold 543 books all hand to hand and had made over $7,000 cash, the money she made was unexpected and she had already made her money back from her print run. 1000 copies had only cost her $2,800 for a 210-page book which was only $2.80 for each copy. She called Stuff as soon as it became dark outside and no one really was out. She even gave the gas station $400 for using their parking lot. They told her she could come back anytime.

"Hello." Stuff answered.

"Hey! You not going to believe this!" she said so excited.

CHAPTER 67

"**W**hat sweetheart?" he asked, smiling also at how happy she was.

"I sold over five hundred books!"

"Damn! That's really good. Are you staying out there or what?"

"Yeah, I think I'mma stay out here for the night. Tonight is a club night. I'mma try to get some sales after the Club is out. I'll be posted up at the Coney Island that everyone goes too."

He laughed. "Ok well be careful. Should I order some more books?"

"Yes, order two thousand. I have the money to pay for them all too."

"Wow. Ok I will do that. The price going to get cheaper the more books you order too."

"I know, well I'm going to call you tomorrow."

"I sent your books to like thirty bookstores. They said they'll get back to you. I think you should get some flyers and posters as well. What you think?"

"That's a good idea."

"Ok I'll have that done for you as well. Call me when you get a chance ok."

"Ok." she said, hanging up. Chase had been calling also so she called him too.

"Hello."

"Hey!"

"What's up beautiful?"

"Nothing, out here in Pontiac selling books." "How

is that going for you?"

"It's going really good. I'm so surprised."

"Am I going to see you on one of them bestsellers list or on one of them big shows?"

"Soon, you will. I have to get people reading it and talking about it."

"That's great Joy. I'm proud of you. When can I see you? I feel like I've been begging you forever."

"I'm going to be down here for a few days so--"

"I'll come there for you." he said.

She was shocked. "Ok, well tomorrow you can come. We'll figure it all out later."

"Ok cool. That's perfect."

CHAPTER 68

After they hung up Joy called up another old friend of hers. His name was Rick and he was around the same age. It rung for a while and he didn't answer but he called her right back.

"Somebody just called Rick?"

"Yes, hey, this is Joy."

"Joy...mmm, which one?"

"Hope's sister!"

"Oh, what's up my baby!? Damn where you been at?"

"I just been trying to get myself together."

"I heard what happened with you and Daniel."

"What you mean? What did you hear?"

"Nothing, just he went to jail and everything went downhill. Nobody even knew where you was at."

"Well I have a different side to that story."

"Hold, hold on real quick." he started looking at Joy's book. A friend of his had bought it earlier from her and he left it at his house. "Hello. Yeah never mind."

"What?" she asked.

"Nothing, I was about to ask you something but never mind."

"What is it Rick?"

"Nothing, I was looking at this book called Turning Tables. The Author on here name Joy also--"

She cut him off. "That's mine! How did you get it?"

"What's yours?"

"That book! I wrote that book!"

"Get the hell out of here!" he said while holding the book looking at it closely.

"I swear!"

"Damn, this is your shit. I'm proud of you Joy. This shit is tight!"

Joy was smiling from ear to ear trying to keep focus as she was driving. "How did you get it?"

"My nigga Ruben left it over here."

"Oh, what are you about to do?" she asked.

"I'm trying to see you. You need to stop playing and fuck back with the kid."

She giggled. "Whatever. You probably got a thousand women after you."

"What do that mean? That ain't got nothing to do with me wanting you."

"You do not want me Rick."

"For real though, when can I see you?"

"I'm in Pontiac right now. What are you doing tonight?"

"I got a party downtown that I'm on my way to in about an hour. You want to go with me? You can sell some books there too."

"Ok. I'll go. Can I come over and get myself ready?"

"Hell yeah, come on."

"Ok, I'll be there in about ten minutes."

CHAPTER 69

They hung up and she arrived minutes later. Her and Rick used to mess around in the past. Daniel had just thought they were friends because that was what Joy swore to, but they had sex in the past. Joy knew what it was with Rick and she never counted on a relationship with him. He was just fun for her to be around

As soon as she parked, she called him to open the door. It was dark out and she had way too much money on her. She didn't want to step out and get robbed.

Rick house was a three bedroom with a small porch in front of it. He had other houses that he rented out, but this was the house he vowed to never sale because his grandmother had left it for him before she passed away. He also had a few Condo's that he rented out to people. Rick was getting money, but you would never know because he wasn't flashy with it. He stayed in a basic house, drove a Buick Lacrosse with tinted windows and dressed very preppy. He was skinny and usually Joy wouldn't go for those type of guy's, but the first time they had sex she was hooked.

As soon as he opened the door for her, he hugged and kissed her while squeezing her booty.

"Stop!" she shouted, snatching away from him.

"Aww, don't be acting brand new. I miss you damn it." he said, smiling as he locked the door.

"Let me get ready and we can talk when I get done. I'll be quick." she said as she went to the bathroom with her small bag. It was weird to her being inside his house because it had been so long.

It wasn't long before she came out of the bathroom wearing a yellow dress that was cut on the sides showing her smooth caramel skin. She wore yellow heels to match and she topped it off with her Tiffany Jewelry Set, the necklace, bracelet and earrings.

"Damn, you still fine as hell!" he said.

"What, I supposed to be ugly now?"

"Naw, but damn. I can't wait until this party over." he said smiling.

"Why? You ain't getting none of this." she said.

"Shiiit!"

"I'm serious. I'm not about to fuck you boy."

"Come on let's go. You talking crazy."

"Rick, you just think you can have your way all the time."

He ignored her. "You want to drive your car?"

"Yeah we can. That's not my car though."

"Oh, well the car you driving."

"This just a little rental. I'm trying to be low key when I come to Pontiac. I don't want to make these hoes mad." she joked.

He laughed, "Where you live at now?" "I

live up north with the white folks." "Oh

ok, That's good. By yourself?" "Yup."

"Look at you. I knew you wasn't broke and doing bad. Everybody was hating on you, like you was just a lil bum."

"t don't matter. Them hoes will see me."

"I know that's right. So, tell me about this book you got. How the hell did you do that?"

They talked all the way to the Club where he was throwing his party at. The line was wrapped around the building when they arrived and Rick told her to valet.

Rick never cared what he rode in because it didn't matter to him. Everyone knew he was the man especially when it came down to getting money legit. He didn't sell drugs but all the money he was making had people thinking that he did.

Everyone was looking at Joy and Rick when they came in with boxes of books. A lot of people was also speaking to both of them, especially Joy because they hadn't seen her in so long. They went right inside and Rick had his people set Joy up a table and she began selling her books to almost everyone in the Club. People that had bought her book earlier bought it again just to support her.

She was signing autographs and taking pictures with everyone that bought a book. They were showing her a lot of love and she was so happy. Of course, she had that big group of haters that wasn't about to buy a book but it didn't matter to Joy. She continued to do her and learned that you cannot expect everyone to buy your book. Just be happy that you sold some.

About an hour later, the Club was packed, and you could barely walk. It was dark and strobe lights and disco lights were flashing everywhere. Everyone was dancing and drinking to the latest song by Future. Rick was back and forth constantly checking on Joy because Phia and two other girls was mean mugging Joy. They had been looking at her since they arrived, and Joy felt it in her stomach that they were going to try something, so the last time Rick checked on her she said something to him.

"Stay close because these bitches look like they about to try something. I know how Phia is."

"You good. Don't sweat it. Even if they do try something, I'm not going to let you get jumped," he said and soon there was a cup a liquor that flew right pass his face landing right on Joy's dress.

"Bitch!" she shouted as she jumped up and tried to get over to them, but Rick held her and Security was holding all the girls. They were all trying to get to each other.

"You dirty ass slut! Fucking your best friend's man!" Phia shouted, kicking her leg out as the muscular security guard was carrying her to the front.

"Tramp bitch!" another girl yelled as she was being held too.

"Dirty Hoe! When I see you, I'm fucking you up!" the other girl shouted over the loud music.

"Let me go!" Joy shouted but she couldn't get loose.

"Calm down!" Rick said.

Everyone had stopped dancing and was watching the scene, but Joy didn't care, she wanted to fight. "Bring them bitches back!" she shouted.

CHAPTER 71

Rick was laughing trying to hold her back. He knew she was a little tipsy from all the small drinks she had drunk. Soon everything had calmed down and Joy was ready to go because her dress was ruined. Rick picked all his money up from the door and told them he would pick the rest up tomorrow and they both left. He drove home and by the time he arrived at his house Joy was all down his pants with her hand and she was kissing all over his lips and neck.

"Hold on, let's go inside." he said, but she had climbed over to his seat and they were kissing. Joy was so horny, and she was craving for some dick, especially his. She pulled her dress right up, sliding her thong to the side and slid his dick inside her wet pussy and started riding him and moaning loudly.

"Damn! Slow down." he said, trying to control her speed by her hips but she was in her zone.

"Oouu baby, I miss you so much!" she moaned out.

After riding him for ten minutes she realized she wasn't about to cum. It was way to uncomfortable inside the car. She soon stopped and was breathing hard on his chest.

"You ready to go inside now?"

She giggled. "Yes, come on." she said, getting out on his side.

"Damn, you got juices all over a nigga." he said looking at his jeans.

He pulled them up and they both went inside and as soon as they got inside, they were back at it. They started in the living room with the lights on. He bent her over his navy blue couch and started pounding her from the back. They then switched positions and Joy begin riding him while he was lying on the couch. She rode him nice and slowly while scratching his chest with her nicely done nails.

Soon he picked her up and carried her to his room. "You bet not drop me." she said giggling wondering how he picked her up because he was so skinny.

"Shut up, I'm not. I got you." he said bumping her head against the wall.

"Oww!" she said.

"Sorry," he said, laughing finally getting to his bed and dropping her gently on it. He then climbed on top of her and began pumping again inside her, eventually making her cum. They had sex all night off and on. When they finally finished it was daylight outside. They were hot and sweaty and when they fell asleep, Joy was at the foot of the bed and Rick was at the head of it. They both were tired but satisfied.

CHAPTER 72

Joy woke up, showered and left around noon. She had herself a great night and the sex had been needed for some time now. But it was time to get back on her grind. After making a stop at the bank and making a big deposit, she headed to the barber shop, the one she was working at some months ago to see if they would sell some of her books for her.

When she walked in, all the guys were looking like they had seen a ghost, "Damn girl, where you been, we thought you was dead," one guy said.

"Dead? Damn, why dead?" she looked surprised.

"Word was, that you were with Pooh when he got killed, people was saying they killed both of you, and some was saying other things," another guy said.

Joy's heart dropped because she had forgot all about that incident and she was instantly feeling like she was in the wrong place. *Fuck, why did I come here,* she thought to herself.

"Other things like what?" she asked.

Joy continued to talk to all the guys about the Pooh situation and she had learned that this was a big deal and a lot of people wanted answers. She had no clue that one of the barbers was calling some of Pooh people up there. She continued to talk to them but made it clear she had no clue about any of that. She told them about her new book and everyone in there bought a copy from her plus gave her a tip, but it was all part of the plan of stalling her out.

By the time Joy walked out of there and was walking to the car, Chase was calling her, this was his third time, but she planned to call him back, she had to call Stuff. She had enough with being around all this drama. She was tired of her name being into all the wrong things.

As she was getting inside her car, she felt someone walk up behind her but before she could turn around, she was being choked out and dragged inside a black van.

Joy opened her eyes and noticed that she was inside a nice huge house that was decorated in white high-quality marble flooring and all the furniture was antique colored a dark grey. Not remembering how she arrived, she tried to move but couldn't because her hands and feet were tied together along with a chair. *Fuck,* she said and tried her hardest to move while looking around until she seen a woman walking towards her.

"Finally up huh?" she said to her. This lady was beautiful, with long hair. She looked like she could be in the Kardashian family, one of the sisters.

"Who are you? And where am I?" Joy asked.

"Relax, Pooh was my husband, that you got killed, and his brother will be here later to talk to you or do whatever he's going to do with you, that depends what you say I guess."

CHAPTER 73

"I swear on my life, my family life that I had nothing to do with that, I will tell you everything that happened, but I promise to god I had nothing to do with that. But yes, I was there, but I did not set that man up. I didn't even know him that well, and I didn't know he was married, I would have never ever."

"Shut up! Save all that for when his brother gets here, I don't want to hear it. They know way more about the murder then I do."

"Please ma'am just don't let them kill me, I really didn't have anything to do with it. Please believe me," Joy said before tears started rolling down her face, but the lady just walked away from her. Minutes later she came back in with a chair and set it next to Joy.

"Were you having sex with my husband?"

"Yes," Joy answered, "But I swear, I had no clue about that man being married."

"Tell me more, how did you meet him?"

"I was working at this barber shop and he would always come in there. I worked at the front desk, so I would always see him. We eventually started going out. And yes, having sex. He never told me he had a wife, girlfriend, kids or anything. But he told me he wanted kids and he would always say I was going to be his baby momma. I'm sorry, no disrespect, I'm just trying to tell you everything I experienced with this man."

"It's ok, continue."

"So, we were going out and stuff, and one day he asked me to come to Atlanta, I agreed. I flew in alone, he bought the ticket, he picked me up and we drove to his house. We weren't in there long before like four guys came in and started pistol whipping him and throwing me all over the place. They took him upstairs and demanded that he give them money. I heard them yelling and still hitting him, because he wasn't cooperating at first, and whatever they started doing to him, he started to tell them things. These guys clearly knew who he was because they were threating to kill his mother and stuff."

"While all that was going on, what was you doing?"

"I was being held at gunpoint by a guy with a black ski mask on, and he kept telling me to relax, and that they weren't there for me. I just kept saying please don't kill me, please don't kill me."

"Then what?"

CHAPTER 74

"It was a lot of rumbling and screaming and they shot him a few times and got what they wanted and came downstairs. They had like 3 or 4 duffle bags and they were telling the dude that was holding me at gunpoint to kill me, but he wouldn't, he just told them to go to the car. He then told me it was my lucky day and to stay away from drug dealers."

"Really?"

"On my life and everyone I love life."

"For some reason I actually believe everything that's coming out your mouth. But I'm not sure if his brother will."

"Please don't let them kill me," Joy started crying again and soon she heard a knock at the door. The wife got up to answer it and it was 6 guys walking in, they all gave the wife hugs and told a few jokes and made their way into the living room where Joy was supposed to be.

"Where is she?" one guy asked.

They all started running through the house looking for her and circling around the house outside. Joy had managed to undo her hands then her feet and she was now hiding inside the closet, shaking and sweating, hoping they wouldn't find her. Sweat was running down her face as she heard them looking through the house for her. When she heard them far away from her, she opened the closet and slowly tiptoed to another closet that was in the hallway, that happened to be like a laundry shoot. It had a rope that was hooked on to a solid box that went upstairs. Joy heard them still scrambling trying to find her, but they were having no luck. She was so scared, and she was ready to make another move. She thought about opening the door and running for her life, but she couldn't stomach up the courage for that. So she grabbed the rope above her and started climbing up the rope while using the wall to make it much easier. For some reason she only heard them downstairs and not upstairs which was good.

By the time she made it up the rope, she was exhausted and out of breath, so she hid under the bed that was in the center of the room until she gained some energy. She could hear them talking, asking the wife questions.

"How long has she been gone for?"

"She was just right here, I don't even understand how she got away that fast. She has to be in here. I had just walked away from her when I answered the door, literally," the wife said.

"This a big ass house, she could be anywhere, you think she's upstairs?"

CHAPTER 75

"*N*o way she's upstairs, I would have seen her go up, I been standing here the whole time, It's only one way up there. Just make sure you guys check all the closets and cabinets down here.

Joy felt a little relief as she slid from under the bed trying not to make any noise. Her plan was to find a good hiding spot and sit there until it was late at night and then she would try to leave. She found a spot inside a guest room closet under some clothes where she planted herself there and waited.

The wife, Pooh brother and his boys had looked all over the house downstairs and in both garages, plus all around the house, even on the next street over, and they couldn't find her anywhere.

As it was getting late, they gave up and left. The wife locked everything up and finally came upstairs, Joy hoped that she was getting ready for bed. She was so ready to get out of there. A couple hours later, Joy didn't hear any noise, and she was ready to make her move.

She stood up and stepped outside the closet without making a loud noise. It was pitch dark, but she could see a little bit because there were no blinds. She lightly began to walk outside the room when she noticed a bat behind the door. She grabbed it and continued to walk. As soon as she got to the hallway, she seen the stairs not too far, so she headed quietly towards them, taking her time with each step as she got lower and lower.

By the time she got to the kitchen, she noticed her purse on the counter, so she grabbed it and headed for the door. Now it was time to make a run for it. She knew once she opened this door, that the alarm was probably going to be going off and she would have to just run for her life. *1....2....3,* She opened it and the alarms were screaming, but Joy took off running as fast as she could across the yard, into the neighbor's yard, then back yard, then over a fence where she was close to a freeway.

A day later

Joy was heading back up to Traverse city on a greyhound bus. Her purse had everything still in it. All she had to do was get a charger for her phone because it was dead. She had called Stuff and let him know that she was heading back up. She talked to Rino and he was good. He had told her that Armoni had survived and was doing much better but Mesha died.

Chase had been calling and was pissed because he had drove all the way down state to see her but she didn't feel like explaining anything to him, so she just blocked his number. He had left 24 voicemails.

CHAPTER 76

F inally, she had made it back to Traverse city and she had told Stuff that someone stole the rental. Joy was still in fear for her life although she got away. She was so happy she was all the way up north, but she wanted so bad to get out of Michigan. She had come close to death too many times and she just wanted to get away.

It had been a week now, and Joy was getting back comfortable with life. She was starting to get back focused and had been spending a lot of time with Stuff. He was teaching her a lot of things and they had become really good friends, but every time they were out in public, people assumed they were together. Tonight, they were at a local bar shooting pool and having drinks.

"If I win this game, you most def taking another shot," she said, laughing at how tipsy she had got Stuff. She was tipsy as well, but she was having so much fun. Stuff knew everyone in there, and they were all treating Joy and Stuff like a queen and king.

"Naw, forget that Joy, you are tripping! I'm done!" Stuff said, with a big smile.

Joy took a shot at the eight ball and missed it, "Damn," she said. "You lucky." She walked back to the high table; they had to take another sip while Stuff was taking his shot. Stuff sure knew how to dress, and Joy always joked and called him DJ Khaled, that's who he looked like to her. "Misssss," she yelled, but it didn't work, Stuff made the rest of the balls go in including the 8 ball, and Joy had to drink.

They had fun as usual and finally leaving to go home, "Are you having company tonight?" she asked.

"I don't think so, why what's up?"

"Just asking."

"You asked for a reason."

"Just was wondering, I was gone sleep in your room tonight."

Stuff was so excited, he had been wanting that since Joy came to his house but he didn't want to be disrespectful to her or A'val so he did what he was asked to do. "About time," he responded with a smile and they both started laughing.

"What that supposed to mean? You always have company, I don't be wanting to interfere in that."

"Stop it, you know damn well it wouldn't be no girls coming over here if you said they couldn't."

"Oh, I got it like that?" she asked.

"You aint know?'

"Zamm zaddy! Naw I ain't know."

They both were tipsy when they got inside Stuff room. It was super clean as always. Joy stripped and jumped right in the bed. It took Stuff a little longer because he was kind of nervous but excited. Finally, after changing into some shorts and turning all the lights off and turning the tv on, he slid in the bed as well and Joy turned over and started talking to him, thanking him for everything he had done for her.

"I appreciate you so much," she whispered, as she touched his face with her soft hands.

"No problem, I told you I got you."

CHAPTER 77

"I know you did, but you like over got me. I feel so safe with you. Thank you so much," she said and kissed him on his lips before he could even say thank you.

"You welcome…that felt good."

"It did," she said and kissed him again, then again, and again until their lips were stuck together, and she was climbing on top of him. He smelled so good to her and she had a different respect for big guys. He smelled better than a lot of guys that weren't even half his size. "You smell so good," she whispered as she continued kissing him and taking his shorts off. She felt his penis pop out, *damn he even got a nice size dick too,* she thought, feeling like she had been living under a rock.

She wanted to really show him how much she appreciated him, so she slid down and put his dick inside her mouth and started sucking and stroking it. "Yes baby, I love it," she heard him say. She sucked and licked his balls until her pussy was dripping wet and then she started riding him.

"Oh my god," she whispered as she rode is dick slowly. "I'm so wet baby," she whispered, grabbing his neck and grinding hard against him, making sure every inch of him was reaching as far as it could inside her. "Baby! Oh my god!" she moaned, "This dick feels sooo good."

"Shiit Joy, I'm going to cum baby."

"Cum inside me baby," she whispered. "Please baby, cum inside me."

Stuff was so turned on by how turned on Joy was for him, he could no longer hold his nut. His dick had swell up so fat and hard and she continued to slide on it more and more until he exploded inside her. "Ahhh shiit!" he grabbed her hips to slow her down, and she leaned on him and started planting soft, wet kisses all over his face, while slightly moving on his dick.

The next morning, Joy was up making breakfast for them both. She served him breakfast in bed and they ate together then got up and took a shower together. Joy had assumed that things would be weird between them, but it was actually better than ever. Nothing was weird and they were still enjoying each other as they continued their routine of visiting his businesses and working towards selling more books.

Joy never went back to sleeping in her own room, Stuff room became her new room, and they were having sex at least twice a day for the next two weeks until Joy wasn't getting her period. Yes, she was pregnant with twins, and Stuff was excited, and Joy was excited as well, especially when Stuff popped the big question with a 6-carat ring in front of all his staff one day when he had taken all 24 of them out to eat. Joy said YES and a week later they were packing up and moving to California. A month later Joy book made the New York Time Bestseller List and she was now working on a movie deal with one of the big film studios in California.

Lock Down Publications and Ca$h Presents assisted publishing packages.

BASIC PACKAGE $499

Editing

Cover Design

Formatting

UPGRADED PACKAGE $800

Typing

Editing

Cover Design

Formatting

ADVANCE PACKAGE $1,200

Typing

Editing

Cover Design

Formatting

Copyright registration

Proofreading

Upload book to Amazon

LDP SUPREME PACKAGE $1,500

Typing

Editing

Cover Design

Formatting

Copyright registration

Proofreading

Set up Amazon account

Upload book to Amazon

Advertise on LDP Amazon and Facebook page

***

Other services available upon request. Additional charges may apply

Lock Down Publications

P.O. Box 944

Stockbridge, GA 30281-9998

Phone # 470 303-9761

Submission Guideline

Submit the first three chapters of your completed manu-script to ldpsubmissions@gmail.com, subject line: Your book's title. The manuscript must be in a .doc file and sent as an attachment. Document should be in Times New Ro-man, double spaced and in size 12 font. Also, provide your synopsis and full contact information. If sending multiple submissions, they must each be in a separate email.

Have a story but no way to send it electronically? You can still submit to LDP/Ca$h Presents. Send in the first three chapters, written or typed, of your completed manuscript to:

LDP: Submissions Dept

Po Box 944

Stockbridge, Ga 30281

DO NOT send original manuscript. Must be a duplicate.

Provide your synopsis and a cover letter containing your full contact information.

Thanks for considering LDP and Ca$h Presents.

Coming Soon from Lock Down Publications/Ca$h Presents

BLOOD OF A BOSS VI

SHADOWS OF THE GAME II

TRAP BASTARD II

By Askari

LOYAL TO THE GAME IV

By T.J. & Jelissa

TRUE SAVAGE VIII

MIDNIGHT CARTEL IV

DOPE BOY MAGIC IV

CITY OF KINGZ III

NIGHTMARE ON SILENT AVE II

THE PLUG OF LIL MEXICO II

CLASSIC CITY II

By Chris Green

BLAST FOR ME III

A SAVAGE DOPEBOY III

CUTTHROAT MAFIA III

DUFFLE BAG CARTEL VII

HEARTLESS GOON VI

By Ghost

A HUSTLER'S DECEIT III

KILL ZONE II

BAE BELONGS TO ME III

TIL DEATH II

By Aryanna

KING OF THE TRAP III

By T.J. Edwards

GORILLAZ IN THE BAY V

3X KRAZY III

STRAIGHT BEAST MODE III

De'Kari

KINGPIN KILLAZ IV

STREET KINGS III

PAID IN BLOOD III

CARTEL KILLAZ IV

DOPE GODS III

Hood Rich

SINS OF A HUSTLA II

ASAD

YAYO V

Bred In The Game 2

S. Allen

THE STREETS WILL TALK II

By Yolanda Moore

SON OF A DOPE FIEND III

HEAVEN GOT A GHETTO III

SKI MASK MONEY III

By Renta

LOYALTY AIN'T PROMISED III

By Keith Williams

I'M NOTHING WITHOUT HIS LOVE II

SINS OF A THUG II

TO THE THUG I LOVED BEFORE II

IN A HUSTLER I TRUST II

By Monet Dragun

QUIET MONEY IV

EXTENDED CLIP III

THUG LIFE IV

By Trai'Quan

THE STREETS MADE ME IV

By Larry D. Wright

IF YOU CROSS ME ONCE III

ANGEL V

By Anthony Fields

THE STREETS WILL NEVER CLOSE IV

By K'ajji

HARD AND RUTHLESS III

KILLA KOUNTY IV

By Khufu

MONEY GAME III

By Smoove Dolla

JACK BOYS VS DOPE BOYS IV

A GANGSTA'S QUR'AN V

COKE GIRLZ II

COKE BOYS II

LIFE OF A SAVAGE V

CHI'RAQ GANGSTAS V

SOSA GANG III

BRONX SAVAGES II

BODYMORE KINGPINS II

By Romell Tukes

MURDA WAS THE CASE III

Elijah R. Freeman

AN UNFORESEEN LOVE IV

BABY, I'M WINTERTIME COLD III

By Meesha

QUEEN OF THE ZOO III

By Black Migo

CONFESSIONS OF A JACKBOY III

By Nicholas Lock

KING KILLA II

By Vincent "Vitto" Holloway

BETRAYAL OF A THUG III

By Fre$h

THE MURDER QUEENS III

By Michael Gallon

THE BIRTH OF A GANGSTER III

By Delmont Player

TREAL LOVE II

By Le'Monica Jackson

FOR THE LOVE OF BLOOD III

By Jamel Mitchell

RAN OFF ON DA PLUG II

By Paper Boi Rari

HOOD CONSIGLIERE III

By Keese

PRETTY GIRLS DO NASTY THINGS II

By Nicole Goosby

LOVE IN THE TRENCHES II

By Corey Robinson

IT'S JUST ME AND YOU II

By Ah'Million

FOREVER GANGSTA III

By Adrian Dulan

GORILLAZ IN THE TRENCHES III

By SayNoMore

THE COCAINE PRINCESS VIII

By King Rio

CRIME BOSS II

Playa Ray

LOYALTY IS EVERYTHING III

Molotti

HERE TODAY GONE TOMORROW II

By Fly Rock

REAL G'S MOVE IN SILENCE II

By Von Diesel

GRIMEY WAYS IV

By Ray Vinci

Available Now

RESTRAINING ORDER I & II

By CA$H & Coffee

LOVE KNOWS NO BOUNDARIES I II & III

By Coffee

RAISED AS A GOON I, II, III & IV

BRED BY THE SLUMS I, II, III

BLAST FOR ME I & II

ROTTEN TO THE CORE I II III

A BRONX TALE I, II, III

DUFFLE BAG CARTEL I II III IV V VI

HEARTLESS GOON I II III IV V

A SAVAGE DOPEBOY I II

DRUG LORDS I II III

CUTTHROAT MAFIA I II

KING OF THE TRENCHES

By Ghost

LAY IT DOWN I & II

LAST OF A DYING BREED I II

BLOOD STAINS OF A SHOTTA I & II III

By Jamaica

LOYAL TO THE GAME I II III

LIFE OF SIN I, II III

By TJ & Jelissa

BLOODY COMMAS I & II

SKI MASK CARTEL I II & III

KING OF NEW YORK I II,III IV V

RISE TO POWER I II III

COKE KINGS I II III IV V

BORN HEARTLESS I II III IV

KING OF THE TRAP I II

By T.J. Edwards

IF LOVING HIM IS WRONG…I & II

LOVE ME EVEN WHEN IT HURTS I II III

By Jelissa

WHEN THE STREETS CLAP BACK I & II III

THE HEART OF A SAVAGE I II III IV

MONEY MAFIA I II

LOYAL TO THE SOIL I II III
By Jibril Williams
A DISTINGUISHED THUG STOLE MY HEART I II & III
LOVE SHOULDN'T HURT I II III IV
RENEGADE BOYS I II III IV
PAID IN KARMA I II III
SAVAGE STORMS I II III
AN UNFORESEEN LOVE I II III
BABY, I'M WINTERTIME COLD I II
By Meesha
A GANGSTER'S CODE I &, II III
A GANGSTER'S SYN I II III
THE SAVAGE LIFE I II III
CHAINED TO THE STREETS I II III
BLOOD ON THE MONEY I II III
A GANGSTA'S PAIN I II III
By J-Blunt
PUSH IT TO THE LIMIT
By Bre' Hayes
BLOOD OF A BOSS I, II, III, IV, V
SHADOWS OF THE GAME
TRAP BASTARD
By Askari
THE STREETS BLEED MURDER I, II & III

THE HEART OF A GANGSTA I II& III

By Jerry Jackson

CUM FOR ME I II III IV V VI VII VIII

An LDP Erotica Collaboration

BRIDE OF A HUSTLA I II & II

THE FETTI GIRLS I, II& III

CORRUPTED BY A GANGSTA I, II III, IV

BLINDED BY HIS LOVE

THE PRICE YOU PAY FOR LOVE I, II ,III

DOPE GIRL MAGIC I II III

By Destiny Skai

WHEN A GOOD GIRL GOES BAD

By Adrienne

THE COST OF LOYALTY I II III

By Kweli

A GANGSTER'S REVENGE I II III & IV

THE BOSS MAN'S DAUGHTERS I II III IV V

A SAVAGE LOVE I & II

BAE BELONGS TO ME I II

A HUSTLER'S DECEIT I, II, III

WHAT BAD BITCHES DO I, II, III

SOUL OF A MONSTER I II III

KILL ZONE

A DOPE BOY'S QUEEN I II III

TIL DEATH

By Aryanna

A KINGPIN'S AMBITON
A KINGPIN'S AMBITION II
I MURDER FOR THE DOUGH
By Ambitious
TRUE SAVAGE I II III IV V VI VII
DOPE BOY MAGIC I, II, III
MIDNIGHT CARTEL I II III
CITY OF KINGZ I II
NIGHTMARE ON SILENT AVE
THE PLUG OF LIL MEXICO II
CLASSIC CITY
By Chris Green
A DOPEBOY'S PRAYER
By Eddie "Wolf" Lee
THE KING CARTEL I, II & III
By Frank Gresham
THESE NIGGAS AIN'T LOYAL I, II & III
By Nikki Tee
GANGSTA SHYT I II &III
By CATO
THE ULTIMATE BETRAYAL
By Phoenix
BOSS'N UP I , II & III
By Royal Nicole
I LOVE YOU TO DEATH
By Destiny J

I RIDE FOR MY HITTA

I STILL RIDE FOR MY HITTA

By Misty Holt

LOVE & CHASIN' PAPER

By Qay Crockett

TO DIE IN VAIN

SINS OF A HUSTLA

By ASAD

BROOKLYN HUSTLAZ

By Boogsy Morina

BROOKLYN ON LOCK I & II

By Sonovia

GANGSTA CITY

By Teddy Duke

A DRUG KING AND HIS DIAMOND I & II III

A DOPEMAN'S RICHES

HER MAN, MINE'S TOO I, II

CASH MONEY HO'S

THE WIFEY I USED TO BE I II

PRETTY GIRLS DO NASTY THINGS

By Nicole Goosby

TRAPHOUSE KING I II & III

KINGPIN KILLAZ I II III

STREET KINGS I II

PAID IN BLOOD I II

CARTEL KILLAZ I II III

DOPE GODS I II

By Hood Rich

LIPSTICK KILLAH I, II, III

CRIME OF PASSION I II & III

FRIEND OR FOE I II III

By Mimi

STEADY MOBBN' I, II, III

THE STREETS STAINED MY SOUL I II III

By Marcellus Allen

WHO SHOT YA I, II, III

SON OF A DOPE FIEND I II

HEAVEN GOT A GHETTO I II

SKI MASK MONEY I II

Renta

GORILLAZ IN THE BAY I II III IV

TEARS OF A GANGSTA I II

3X KRAZY I II

STRAIGHT BEAST MODE I II

DE'KARI

TRIGGADALE I II III

MURDAROBER WAS THE CASE I II

Elijah R. Freeman

GOD BLESS THE TRAPPERS I, II, III

THESE SCANDALOUS STREETS I, II, III

FEAR MY GANGSTA I, II, III IV, V

THESE STREETS DON'T LOVE NOBODY I, II

BURY ME A G I, II, III, IV, V

A GANGSTA'S EMPIRE I, II, III, IV

THE DOPEMAN'S BODYGAURD I II

THE REALEST KILLAZ I II III

THE LAST OF THE OGS I II III

Tranay Adams

THE STREETS ARE CALLING

Duquie Wilson

MARRIED TO A BOSS I II III

By Destiny Skai & Chris Green

KINGZ OF THE GAME I II III IV V VI VII

CRIME BOSS

Playa Ray

SLAUGHTER GANG I II III

RUTHLESS HEART I II III

By Willie Slaughter

FUK SHYT

By Blakk Diamond

DON'T F#CK WITH MY HEART I II

By Linnea

ADDICTED TO THE DRAMA I II III

IN THE ARM OF HIS BOSS II

By Jamila

YAYO I II III IV

A SHOOTER'S AMBITION I II

BRED IN THE GAME

By Robert Baptiste

NEW TO THE GAME I II III

MONEY, MURDER & MEMORIES I II III

By Malik D. Rice

LIFE OF A SAVAGE I II III IV

A GANGSTA'S QUR'AN I II III IV

MURDA SEASON I II III

GANGLAND CARTEL I II III

CHI'RAQ GANGSTAS I II III IV

KILLERS ON ELM STREET I II III

JACK BOYZ N DA BRONX I II III

A DOPEBOY'S DREAM I II III

JACK BOYS VS DOPE BOYS I II III

COKE GIRLZ

COKE BOYS

SOSA GANG I II

BRONX SAVAGES

BODYMORE KINGPINS

By Romell Tukes

LOYALTY AIN'T PROMISED I II

By Keith Williams

QUIET MONEY I II III

THUG LIFE I II III

EXTENDED CLIP I II

A GANGSTA'S PARADISE

By Trai'Quan

THE STREETS MADE ME I II III

By Larry D. Wright

THE ULTIMATE SACRIFICE I, II, III, IV, V, VI

KHADIFI

IF YOU CROSS ME ONCE I II

ANGEL I II III IV

IN THE BLINK OF AN EYE

By Anthony Fields

THE LIFE OF A HOOD STAR

By Ca$h & Rashia Wilson

THE STREETS WILL NEVER CLOSE I II III

By K'ajji

CREAM I II III

THE STREETS WILL TALK

By Yolanda Moore

NIGHTMARES OF A HUSTLA I II III

By King Dream

CONCRETE KILLA I II III

VICIOUS LOYALTY I II III

By Kingpen

HARD AND RUTHLESS I II

MOB TOWN 251

THE BILLIONAIRE BENTLEYS I II III

REAL G'S MOVE IN SILENCE

By Von Diesel

GHOST MOB

Stilloan Robinson

MOB TIES I II III IV V VI

SOUL OF A HUSTLER, HEART OF A KILLER I II

GORILLAZ IN THE TRENCHES I II

By SayNoMore

BODYMORE MURDERLAND I II III

THE BIRTH OF A GANGSTER I II

By Delmont Player

FOR THE LOVE OF A BOSS

By C. D. Blue

MOBBED UP I II III IV

THE BRICK MAN I II III IV V

THE COCAINE PRINCESS I II III IV V VI VII

By King Rio

KILLA KOUNTY I II III IV

By Khufu

MONEY GAME I II

By Smoove Dolla

A GANGSTA'S KARMA I II III

By FLAME

KING OF THE TRENCHES I II III

by GHOST & TRANAY ADAMS

QUEEN OF THE ZOO I II

By Black Migo

GRIMEY WAYS I II III

By Ray Vinci

XMAS WITH AN ATL SHOOTER

By Ca$h & Destiny Skai

KING KILLA

By Vincent "Vitto" Holloway

BETRAYAL OF A THUG I II

By Fre$h

THE MURDER QUEENS I II

By Michael Gallon

TREAL LOVE

By Le'Monica Jackson

FOR THE LOVE OF BLOOD I II

By Jamel Mitchell

HOOD CONSIGLIERE I II

By Keese

PROTÉGÉ OF A LEGEND I II III

LOVE IN THE TRENCHES

By Corey Robinson

BORN IN THE GRAVE I II III

By Self Made Tay

MOAN IN MY MOUTH

By XTASY

TORN BETWEEN A GANGSTER AND A GENTLEMAN

By J-BLUNT & Miss Kim

LOYALTY IS EVERYTHING I II

Molotti

HERE TODAY GONE TOMORROW

By Fly Rock
PILLOW PRINCESS
By S. Hawkins
NAÏVE TO THE STREETS
By A. Roy Milligan
BOOKS BY LDP'S CEO, CA$H

TRUST IN NO MAN
TRUST IN NO MAN 2
TRUST IN NO MAN 3
BONDED BY BLOOD
SHORTY GOT A THUG
THUGS CRY
THUGS CRY 2
THUGS CRY 3
TRUST NO BITCH
TRUST NO BITCH 2
TRUST NO BITCH 3
TIL MY CASKET DROPS
RESTRAINING ORDER
RESTRAINING ORDER 2
IN LOVE WITH A CONVICT
LIFE OF A HOOD STAR
XMAS WITH AN ATL SHOOTER

www.ingramcontent.com/pod-product-compliance
Lightning Source LLC
Chambersburg PA
CBHW070456260626
47161CB00004B/1332